A Hard Man is Good To Find!

James W. Lewis

TPC BOOKS

The Pantheon Collective (TPC)
www.pantheoncollective.com

The Pantheon Collective (TPC)
P.O. Box 799
Santa Cruz, CA 95061

ISBN: 978-0-9827193-4-3 (Paperback)
ISBN: 978-0-9827193-5-0 (Ebook)

Printed in United States of America

Cover: Designed by Marion Designs
Interior: Designed by Stephanie Casher

To Mommy

Acknowledgments

Wow! I can't believe I'm doing this again a year later almost to the day! And just like last year, it's three in the morning and I'm blazing the keyboards, yawning and popping ear drums while listening to old school 80s Hip Hop. You can never go wrong with Dougie Fresh and Rakim!

It's been a wild ride navigating the crowded world of publishing and promoting indie books the past year. Twitter, Facebook, interviews (print, online, and radio), traveling, book reviews, blogs, contests, bookstores, signings—*man!* Enough to make your brain cave in!

But 'cha know what? I'm lovin' every minute of it. ☺

Hard work pays off! Can you believe TPC has won several awards since we debuted my first book *Sellout* in June 2010? Check it out:

2011 International Book Awards Winner
(for the *African American Fiction* category)

2011 National Black Book Festival — Best New Author Award

2011 Indie Excellence Award Finalist

2011 Next Generation Indie Book Award Finalist

*2010 AALBC Best Book Trailer of the Year (3rd place)***

2010 Best Reviewed Books — Urban Reviews

Didn't I say it's been a wild ride? But of course, TPC couldn't have done it without a little (okay, a LOT) of help along the way, so J-Dub would like to thank the following:

As always, I'd like to thank the Man upstairs. As you can probably tell I'm working this gift He's given me to the max!

Thank you, Mom! Who knew I would still be chugging along on this writing journey after you put me on restriction a million years ago, forcing young "Jr." to write short stories? I know I didn't, but of course, they don't say "Mom knows best" for nothin'.

I thanked most folks individually in my last book, so this time around, I'm gonna go with "bulk" thank yous: to my brothers, the Garrards, Cashers, my Circle of Usual Suspects (you know who you are), the male authors I look up to, and industry friends—I appreciate ya'll!

To Claudia Menza: You were the first one to believe in this project, and your feedback has been priceless. Thank you for giving this book a chance. I am forever grateful.

I've also collected a truckload of new friends! Thanks to all my Twitter followers and Facebook friends, especially the frequent posters to my Questions of the Day. Man, we have some of the craziest discussions on my Facebook wall! I always learn something new every time I post a question. LOL. Thanks for participating!

To the book clubs: Man, I've gotten a ton of love from these "book soldiers," always treating me like a King. It's a strange (but great) feeling when book clubs break down my characters to the molecules, analyzing scenes in the book like a forensic scientist at a crime location. As an author, to see a group of ladies in a picture holding your book … priceless. Book clubs are truly a new author's greatest ally because they drum up that elusive buzz factor. Like a disc jockey for a new musician, book clubs get the "word out on the streets" for authors.

On that note, I'd like to thank the following book clubs:

Urban Divas
Sisters Turning Pages
Sisterhood Connection
Sisters United
Sistaz in Sync
Sistaz of Distinction
Las Vegas Newbians
Kinky Hair Readers
Mocha Socialites
Mocha Mixers
Sista's Bookclub (Sbsc)
African Violets
Sistahs of Urban Literature
Sistas' Thoughts from Coast to Coast (STCC)

Thank you, Gwen Richardson! For years you've been a huge proponent for African American entrepreneurs through Cushcity, and I am extremely honored to have won The Best New Author Award for the

2011 National Black Book Festival. Thanks for all you do to support new authors. I love your insightful posts on Facebook, too. ☺

Thanks to Candra Jolly for featuring my article and beefcake picture in *Kraze* magazine! LOL Congrats on getting *Kraze* to the masses. If you love articles for female enjoyment and guys all GQ'd out (some half-naked, some not), check out this magazine!

To Marcus Books, Bookshop Santa Cruz, & CSUMB Student Bookstore: Thanks for carrying *Sellout!* Hope you take this one on, too! Thanks also to Cabrillo College and UCSC for letting TPC speak to your creative writing classes!

To my TPC partner and friend Omar: Thanks again for your thoughtful insight on *A Hard Man*. I appreciate you taking the time to read and critique this book and once again, I feel it's a stronger product because of you. I only hope I was able to return the favor with *One Blood*.

By the way, *One Blood* is TPC's next book. Watch out for it!

Last but never least, to Stephanie: I believe you are (and always have been) someone who shares the same heartbeat and rhythm—a true soul mate. It's a word I almost never use, so you know that's saying a lot (smile)! Thanks for always being in my corner. I feel like no matter how many times I've been knocked down, you're always there yelling in my ear, telling me how to bob and weave through this crazy life we've created. *Cheese Alert*: I feel like Rocky and you're Mickey and Adrian rolled into one. I only hope I'm doing the same. DWK loves you!

And if I forgot anybody, I'll get ya in the next one! In the meantime, hit me up anytime at james_wil_lew@yahoo.com. Check out my websites at www.jameswlewis.com and www.pantheoncollective.com (TPC). The TPC website has tons of information for newbie authors!

Thank you ALL! I hope you enjoy my sophomore effort A HARD MAN IS GOOD TO FIND!

Peace and love,

James W. Lewis
The Pantheon Collective (TPC)
15 May 2011

Chapter 1

Girl, I need to holla at you for a minute 'cause a sista has serious issues. Well, actually, one *major* issue. You're probably gonna look at me like I'm crazy after I tell you all of this. You don't mind sittin' back for a minute while I spill it, do you? I'll tell you straight up, I've been known to yack folk's ears off. Mouth be running at times, so you might wanna grab a caffé latte and somethin' to munch on, all right?

Well, my issue comes in a dark chocolate-delight package of 100 percent testosterone ... *damn* ... with a body built like an NFL wide receiver, firm rock-hard Terrell Owens-ish ass ... *lawd! And* he makes damn near six-figures as a computer analyst!

Okay, okay. Stop right there. You probably got your lips all twisted up, rolling your eyes, about to slam the book on me and what not. Talkin' 'bout, "yeah, right, here we go *again*. The men in these books are always off-the-charts fine." I hear you and all, but I'm telling you, it's true!

I'm talkin' bleach-white teeth, a damn near Barry White voice, and the smoothest bald head I've had the pleasure of rubbing my hands on. Quite simply, the man can trigger a dozen micro-orgasms with a simple smile and "hello."

But even though he's an Ebony Man of the Decade candidate, I'm debating on seeing him again. I just don't know if I can stand him anymore, let alone make our relationship work. That, girlfriend, is the issue.

You'll see what I'm talkin' 'bout later on. But before I say anything more about him, let me tell you the crazy scenarios I found myself in before I met him.

I hadn't been to a nightclub in months. Just got tired of the scene, ya know, same ol' faces, same ol' routine, same ol' bullshit. Every time I stepped foot inside a weekend hot spot, I felt like worm bait among a sea of piranhas. Screw that. I'm nobody's bait, so I kept my ass home.

Don't get me wrong, I loved the attention men showered on me. What woman wouldn't? But the shit just got old after a while, ya know. Well, at least for me it did—especially since I knew most men in meat markets disguised as nightclubs just wanted a piece of my sirloin steak for a midnight snack. Horny toad freaks.

It got to a point where weekend dates with Netflix and pizza became the norm for my oh-so solo life. Not that I was complaining. Just got used to that pattern.

One Friday after work, I found my girlfriend Charlotte standing against the door of my Subaru, blocking my entry. The way she had her arms spread against the window glass, I thought she was hiding something.

This heifer done lost her mind, I thought. I set my hands on my hips and said, "Ho, what the hell are you doing?"

She stared at me with beady, dark-brown eyes. Wrinkling her forehead, she crunched her eyebrows together, trying to look mean and shit. Had this crazy look like a woman determined to make a point.

Charlotte took in a deep breath. "Look, Michelle. I've been trying to get you to go out with me for I don't know how long now. I'm tired of my girl tellin' me she don't wanna go out. You know I don't have long before my next pregnancy test has that plus sign on it."

I shook my head. How this girl gonna play the pregnancy card? Charlotte and her husband, Greg, had been putting in work for the past two months to knock her up. She was trying to get the clubbin' out of her system before the nine-month wobble.

Charlotte rambled on. "You need to get your ass out and have some fun. Why you all stuck in your apartment all the damn time, messin' around on Facebook? You know I don't like hangin' with—"

"Aw'ight, aw'ight!" I threw my hands up in surrender. "Damn! I'll go out with you tonight!"

As you can see, I didn't put up much of a fight. I had actually gotten the itch to wiggle it on the floor again, but let Charlotte think she had convinced me.

Homechick adjusted her stance and exhaled with an exaggerated "you rescued me" look. "Woo!" she said. "Thank you! 'Bout time!"

She wiped her forehead, even though it didn't show a lick of sweat. So damn silly. Always acting the fool, crackin' me up. That's my girl, though. Best friend for five years.

After we ironed out the details, I drove to El Cajon, got my hair braided, then headed home. I looked good with my shoulder-length braids, but after four hours of my hairdresser twisting my hair and yanking my scalp, mini-headaches pounded my cranium with the throb knob on high. I thought about lazing in front of the TV and calling it a night, but didn't want Charlotte having a fit. I took a couple of aspirin and sucked it up. Couldn't punk out on my girl—I'd never hear the end of it.

At my Mission Valley apartment, hip-hop jams from 90.3 restored the boogie in my hips and snap in my fingers. I ordered homegirl in the mirror to have a good time tonight.

I showered, ransacked the closet, and grabbed the tan mini dress that cuddles all my goodies. I had to make sure the brothas checked me out until their eyes hurt, ya know? And, shoot, why not put my hourglass on blast? My mama gave it to me!

I wiped the dust off my brown pumps, slapped on a touch of blush, and coated my thick lips with Red Seduction. A dab of Chanel perfume around my neck, arms, and the slit between my two babies blessed my body with a classy fragrance.

Once I put in my diamond earrings, I checked out the finished product in the mirror. Hell, I shot through the Richter scale, I'm not gonna lie. I felt like a woman about to break a few hearts and crush an army of egos with my fine self. It had been a while since I got dressed up like this for a night on the town.

Charlotte came by my apartment around 10:45 and we rode in her black Navigator. My girl rocked a black halter and purple skirt with a slit on the side. Never one to wear a lot of makeup, she only needed a hint of diamond-shine lip gloss to complement her baby-smooth, honey-coated complexion. Her bump-n-curl showed every bit the hundred or so dollars she paid for it.

That's one lucky girl. She can go to a meat market with her single friend looking so fresh and so clean and her husband doesn't even flinch. Greg's a mature, laid-back brotha who's got it together— a sales supervisor during the day, aspiring novelist at night. Charlotte's clubbing doesn't sweat him 'cause he *knows* where his wife will be by two in the morning. Of course, her three-to-four hour absence gives him plenty of quiet time to bang out the novel he's been working on for half a year. The ultimate marital win-win.

We got to the club fifteen minutes later. Soon as I heard Usher's jam "OMG" vibrating the room, it was on! As we made our way to the bar, brothas eyed Charlotte and me as if we were two plates of Roscoe's chicken and waffles. A few brave ones stepped to us, trying to get their Mack-Daddy-Pimp game on. The bling from Charlotte's two-carat rock clearly publicized her marital status, but some dudes still tried to slip weak lines like "Where yo' man at?" or "Why he let a fine woman like you out by yo' self?" Same ol' bullshit. Fools that pushed up on me too hard saw the back of my head or palm of my hand.

Charlotte and I found a table by the dance floor and sat down amongst a pack of horny two-legged hounds. Among the canines, I met my first mistake.

Chapter 2

Reject #1

Gerald. Now that was one bold nucca.

While I babysat her drink, I watched Charlotte on the floor with this Paul Pierce lookin' dude ... you know, the basketball player. As I sipped on an Apple Martini while swaying to an Alicia Keys cut, I caught a few brothas targeting me, but none moved my way. Probably waiting for that liquid courage to creep into their systems so they could throw me a tired line.

Fools were *so* obvious, licking their lips and stroking their chins as they stared at my legs, probably scheming up ways on how to "dance" between them. Damn shame. I say again, horny toad freaks.

Right as Alicia's song ended, the DJ broke it down with Jodeci's "Love U 4 Life," one of my all-time favorite slow jams. I guess Charlotte wasn't feelin' the song 'cause she unwrapped herself from "Paul," waved him off, and walked back to the table. Had his ass standing on the floor, palms in the air, looking like "huh?" She was wrong for that. Funny, but wrong.

I felt a tap on my shoulder and turned to find a brotha in a smooth cream-colored suit and derby standing over me.

He leaned down, lips brushing my ear. "Would you like to dance?"

Nice and polite, like a true gentleman. Sometimes, that's all it takes. Say it right, do it right, you in there, ya know? Can't be grabbing my arm all rough like you payin' property taxes on me and shit, spewing some mess like "yo, shorty, you wanna dance?" Damn, I hate when guys call me "shorty."

I glanced at Charlotte and she waved me on with that "go 'head" look in her eye. We then swapped purse-watching duties.

So I said to him, "Sure."

I stood up and he took my hand as we edged toward the floor. He looked pretty nice in that fly suit. Not only that, the brotha sported my favorite men's fragrance: CK One cologne. I can inhale that masculine mist all day *every* day.

After telling me his name, of course he tried to drop game on me, sayin' I looked fine, smelled good—that kinda stuff. You know brothas be gettin' their Mack on at warp speed minutes before the club lights come back on, huh? Ha! Shoot, most men will say and do anything to make sure they end the night with some girl's face buried in a pillow.

After a couple of songs, I got a better look at Gerald. Hmmm, not bad. Clean cut. No facial hair. Bald fade. Dark-brown skin. He wasn't Taye Diggs or anything, but definitely doable.

We exchanged numbers. To my surprise, he didn't roll up on me much, either, trying to push his luck. He took my number, kissed my hand, and stepped out. Pretty smooth.

Charlotte and I left sometime after midnight and in minutes I slipped knee-deep in some rapid eye movement, girl. Knocked the hell *out*, you hear me? The drinks and late hours had me damn near comatose by the time Charlotte dropped me off. I hadn't stayed up that long in a minute, so ya girl couldn't hang. I'm not ashamed to admit it, either.

What I *am* ashamed to admit is that I messed with Gerald. *This* fool!

Gerald and I kicked it for about three weeks after we met at the club. We did the safe stuff like dinner and movies—even checked out a preseason NBA game. If not with Charlotte, Gerald became my back-up buddy.

I liked Gerald. He was funny and all, a gentleman at times— which is why I'm still shocked at what that fool did. Or *tried* to do.

One night after catching a play in downtown San Diego, a sista decided to *not* roll home solo. Truth be told, I had an itch that needed some scratching, so it was time to close the loop with Gerald. Even though I didn't feel any love connection, I had a feeling Gerald would make a fine D.A.D.

What? You know what D.A.D. stands for! Every single sista I know has an after-hours "friend" on speed dial, aka Dial-A-Dick. You know, the plumber you call when you need a hard snake to unclog your main valve in the middle of the night. Don't front, if you ain't got one, you know somebody who does.

Anyway, after he strapped on a Trojan, he went to work, doin' the doggy style thing. It had been a minute since a man stroked my kitty. Felt damn good, too, and I knew it wouldn't have been long before I hit the big O. Everything was kosher—until Gerald tried to stick his bat into the *wrong* dugout.

Yeah, you heard me right. Apparently Gerald got tired of the front door and tried to break in through the *back*.

And, no, it's not like he slipped out then tried to hit the right target again. Homeboy knew exactly where he was aiming that thing.

"Oh *hells* no!" I screamed.

Now don't get me wrong, I'm down for some agreed upon freaky-deaky, but not some unapproved *sneaky* freaky deaky. And this here? Sneaky as they come. Ain't no damn way, let me tell you. Penile enemas will *never* become a dish on Michelle's menu, you hear me? Not that kind of party, Charlie. I guess Captain Ahab wanted to conquer the seas by sailing through uncharted channels. Well, that fool rocked the wrong boat.

I yanked my butt forward. "Muthafucka, what the hell do you think you're doin'?"

He tilted his head, looking like little Gary Coleman, talkin' 'bout, "Huh? Whatchu talkin' 'bout?"

Yeah, he wanted to do some "Different Strokes" all right. But not with this chick.

"You know what the hell I'm talkin' 'bout!" I yelled. "You do that shit again and I will Lorena Bobbit your ass, you hear me?"

Can you believe this fool got mad? Rolling his eyes, making "pssst" sounds and shit. "Aw'ight, aw'ight," he said. "My bad."

With that settled, we went back to the task at hand. Face in the pillow, I assumed the position once again.

Now you're probably wondering why I kept on after he tried to pull a sneak move like that, right? Shoot, why do you think? A sista needed some, simple as that.

But not *that* bad.

Granted, he was working it, and, girl, I was definitely feeling it. Moans reached a high pitch. Sweat saturated my pillow. My arms jerked, thighs shook, cries grew louder. A man hadn't taken me to my peak in months, and damn it, I almost got there! I was about to explode when...

That dirty muthafucka pulled out and tried to dig inside my booty hole again.

No more of that bullshit. I swung my body to the side, flipped over, and karate-kicked that fool square in his chest. Yes, I did! The Bionic Woman couldn't have moved as fast.

"Nigga, I done told you, I ... you know what ... get out! Get the fuck out! Now!" I *never* drop the N-word, and I'm ashamed that I did, but I had reached the peak of pisstivity.

I don't know if he thought negotiating would help or what 'cause this idiot had his palms up, talkin' 'bout, "Chill out, woman! I'm sayin' though, if you just let me do my thang, I think you'll like it. I did it with these three other females and they all liked it. I got more rubbers in case it rips. You need some lubricant, huh?"

My jaw dropped. Oh, no he didn't. *More rubbers? Lubricant?*

That triflin', ignorant, wannabe pooper scooper actually went there. Ugh! I swear I felt steam billowing out my ears. And like I *really* needed an inventory of the nasty ass hoes he'd run through. Disgusting!

I caught another reflex and tried to kick his nuts out his back, but he sidestepped my hot foot. That fool's lucky. I highly doubt kids would've been in his future if I'd made contact.

"What the hell?" he yelled. "Damn, I thought you was a freak! Kickin' me in my chest and shit. You trippin'! Aw'ight, aw'ight, I'm out."

Can you believe that? *This* nasty fool thought I was a freak. What the hell kind of freak was he thinkin'?

Since he slammed my front door, I haven't seen nor heard from Gerald. Hope I never do. Man, what a wild night. How do you even face a person after that? You're right, you can't! Guess I need to tape a "Do Not Enter" sign on my booty for future reference.

Girl, I wish I could say my love life took a turn for the better after the Booty Bandit, but it really didn't.

Chapter 3

Reject #2

Lawrence. The reverse of big things come in small packages.

With the whirlwind blur of the holidays and visiting family, I hadn't done much night life mingling. I blame that on Gerald the Anal Invader. After him, the idea of socializing with the weaker sex lost all appeal. Then New Years rolled around and I decided to end my short boycott of men. I got back in the game with a hair and fashion show at the Doubletree hotel not too far from my apartment. Charlotte and I went. That's where I met Lawrence.

I really can't say what I saw in him. Maybe the boyish smile turned me on, despite the gap between his top front teeth? Maybe the "Nawlins" accent rang my bell? Hmmm ... don't know, really. Maybe because he smelled good. Or maybe I just needed a "tune-up" and all fluids checked.

I kicked it with him for about two weeks. Being in the Navy, he was out to sea at least five out of those fourteen days; otherwise, I probably would've kicked his butt to the curb sooner. I actually thought this one had the potential to go the distance, but it only took one night to mess up that fantasy. Yep, just like that.

One Saturday afternoon, Lawrence invited me to a cookout at Mission Beach Park. The January weather was unusual, even for San

Diego—clear skies, sixty-degree weather, light breeze. He played basketball most of the time, while a few other females and I gossiped over a game of Dominoes.

Lawrence had done a great job scoping out all the Cajun treats here on the West Side, and dinner was all Louisiana-style dishes— gumbo, jambalaya, boudin. We tore that stuff up, boy, *and* got our drink on. I must've downed at least five bottles of Heineken in a four-hour period, a little much for me. Lawrence became a funnel, knocking back about eight of them bad boys. I had a good time, though.

I admit, he shouldn't have driven at all—and I shouldn't have let him—but we managed to get back to my neck of the woods in his Explorer. Yes, *I know! Very* dumb move on my part. We were pretty lucky the guys in blue didn't cross our path.

But the bad decisions continued since the Heinekens drowned a few of Lawrence's and *too* many of my brain cells. Shoot, he even stopped at Ralph's grocery store to pick up *more* brain cell killing booze. I ain't gonna lie, I told him to bring a sista back a bottle of wine. I felt just about right, but wasn't quite there yet.

We got to my apartment a few minutes later. A sista has only one TV, so we went straight to the bedroom. While he fiddled with my DVDs, I dipped into the kitchen and returned with two glasses.

"I'ma put in one of these old Def Jam DVDs, aw'ight?" he said.

I handed him a glass. "Go 'head."

We lost our shoes, laid upright against the headboard of my bed, and watched the DVD. Lawrence had this high-pitched cluck disguised as laughter. I didn't even have to watch the DVD to get my giggle on. Listening to him was comedy enough.

Yeah, we were chillaxin', all hugged up and comfy. Next thing you know, my lips touched his and ... well, what can I say? One thing led to another.

I think the last glass of wine murdered the rest of my brain cells 'cause all I wanted was him and "it." Normally I wouldn't have any man's funky ass on my bed after playing basketball, dried sweat caked on his body and all, but at that point, I was like "fuck it."

He unzipped my pants, working two fingers between my legs, my sugar walls all nice, wet, and more than ready. "You got any ... *damn* ... any condoms?" I asked.

"Oh, fo' sho'."

This fool. That "fo' sho' " crap was killing the mood. I admit, the taste and smell of Heineken-breath didn't help either, but I had it, too—and like I said, I was in "fuck it" mode. A let's-just-do-this-and-I'll-deal-with-the-consequences-later type thing.

You've been there before, right? I'm sure.

Anyway, when I thought I would explode from the finger action, Lawrence jumped out of bed.

Trying to catch my breath, I sat up. "Where you goin'?"

He replied, "Gotta go to the bath—"

Clu-clunk!

Girl!

That fool's shorts had wrapped around his ankles, tangling his feet. After he slammed into my bathroom door, he bitch-slapped the tile floor with his belly. I had to cover my mouth 'cause I almost screamed. Drunk ass. It took him a while to figure out how to stand again. Bangin' against my toilet, the wall, towel rack, my little trash can—damn!

"Don't be messin' up my bathroom, now," I said.

He finally stood upright. After struggling with the doorknob, he closed the door.

With the remote, I turned off the DVD and switched the channels, landing on MTV2 and watching an old school Missy Elliot video. I noticed the clock on my dresser said sumn' like 9:32. I lay with my shirt still on but everything else on display, so I covered myself with the sheets. Alcohol still had a sista somewhat woozy, but now that he had revved me up, I was ready to go at it—until I heard this wretched sound:

"Brrraaaatt!"

I whipped my head around, face all crunched up. Didn't process the noise at first, then I heard it again.

Aw damn.

This fool was sitting on *my* toilet playing the fart symphony. Funking up my Mango Mandarin fragrance, too!

Ew! I smacked my tongue and shook my head, turning up the TV volume to muffle the nasty butt blasts vibrating from my bathroom. He sounded like a car with a bad engine up in there.

Cradling my head in my hand, I watched another old rap video, ho-humming along, ya know, thinking twice about my eventual rendez-screw with Lawrence while his asshole flapped and sputtered. He needed to kill that noise quick.

But that's nothing compared to what he did when he came out.

Right when he opened the door, they took it back with that Juvenile song "Back That Azz Up." Leftover alcohol must have twirked a brotha's system 'cause that fool turned his back to me and wobbled like those ghetto hoochies on the TV! I kid you not, girl. Homeboy had his booty cheeks clappin' like a standing ovation.

I was stu-pe-fied, you hear me? This jackass—emphasis on "ass"—was standing butt naked in front of my TV trying to drop it like it's hot!

My jaw dropped, eyes so wide they damn near popped out the sockets. I just lay there, watching this low-budget exotic dancer. Lawd, was I that desperate?

Then this fool did a spin move and faced me. Fake ass Ginuwine started doin' the Butterfly. Yes, the *Butterfly!* Remember that ancient dance? He had a goofy ass Sweet Dick Willie look, too, 'bout to break a sista off with a lil' sumn' sumn'. Ha! Damn shame. I guess he felt good about finally getting some coochie and the fool wanted to celebrate. Probably been a while. The way he was acting, I could see why.

Rotating his legs to the beat, homeboy disappeared in his Butterfly zone. He even closed his eyes. Meanwhile, my eyes traveled downward.

And I almost passed the fuck out.

A scream rushed from the bottom of my throat, but I cuffed a palm over my lips and captured it in my mouth. What I saw scared the hell out of me. Actually, what I *didn't* see scared the hell out of me.

I only saw *bush.*

I had to rub my knuckles against my eye sockets *hard!* Blinked a few times, too. My vision's not 20-20, but it ain't 20-200, either. I saw nothing that should have been hanging down, ya know?

Then he opened his mouth again. "You like this, don't you? Yeah, you fixin' to get a taste of this sausage meat heah."

Sausage meat?

I leaned forward, trying to find the pig in the blanket behind a crop full of hay. I swear, I wanted to put out an APB—All Penis

Bulletin—for that brotha 'cause the dingaling was *lack-ing!* Can you say, "extra belly button?"

Damn shame. How you gon' bring the buns to the party and forget the meat?

At first I shook my head 'cause I kinda felt sorry for him. But as he continued on with his solo bump and grind routine, something stirred inside me. I lowered my eyebrows, balling up the sheets with my fists.

I was getting pissed! Not because he blocked the TV, but because he had the nerve to bring that hairy toothpick into my house! With me hornier than an out-of-work porn star, I wasn't sure that little thing was gonna cut it. Part of me wanted to get up, slip on my Reeboks, and drive to his mama and daddy's house so I could backslap them for making a son with a pencil dick.

Alcohol had jacked me up, now. Don't mind me. I'm just being silly.

Anyway, after about a minute of his old-school Bobby Brown humpin' mid-air act, Lawrence strolled toward the bed. Crazy as it sounds, something stirred inside me again. As repulsed, angry, and drunk as I was, I still wanted some penile refreshment. Yeah, I know it don't make much sense. A cocktail of hormones and alcohol strips away *all* good sense.

So against my better judgment, I got ready to do the damn thing. By the time he unwrapped the Trojan—I still had *some* good sense, now—I had convinced myself Lawrence held special talent in that little wand of his. Like they say, it ain't the size of the bat, it's how you swing it. Yup, I had psyched myself up. Lawrence was fixin' to service me with a smile, right?

Wrong!

Before he disappeared inside I caught this lopsided, Charlie Brown-lookin' grin. Damn! I have never seen a man so happy to get some coochie!

He was moving all around, trying to work it, but did his thing like a ballet dancer with a broken foot. I wanted to ask if it was in all the way, but stopped myself. No need to make a brotha feel any smaller than he already was. I happened to glance over at the clock. 9:45.

Within seconds—yes, *seconds*—he started gruntin' like a pig. So damn funny. For a moment he reminded me of kindergarten 'cause he broke down the vowels for a sista, talkin' 'bout, "Aaaa ... eeee ... iiii!"—he threw in a "damn" and "shit" here and there, then returned with, "oohhh ... uuuuuuu!"

Then homeboy got ta twitchin' and shakin'. He straight went spasmodic on me, girl. Wiggling all around, shooting spit missiles all up on my forehead. Ugh! I know my stuff can blow a brotha's mind—but good enough to make him convulse?

I just stared at this fool, not even into it, thinking he was fixin' to blow up. Had my legs all spread, like he was Dr. Long Stroke or somebody.

Yeah, right.

His eyes got so wide they looked like cue balls with black dots in the middle. He reminded me of the "Thriller" video. Ha! Homeboy needed an exorcism with all those ugly ass fuck faces, girl. His arms even jerked all out of whack and shit. I thought the song "Planet Rock" was playing the way he pop-locked.

While focused on the fun only *he* was having, you *know* what happened next. With one last grunt, growl and grind combination—*splash!*

All done.

Damn. You woulda thought he'd just run a marathon the way he collapsed on my chest, heaving and struggling for air. I just lay there, staring at the ceiling, wondering how the hell I was gonna get this fool off me.

I released a long sigh, then turned to the clock. 9:46.

And it had *just* clicked to that.

Ain't that some shit? Couldn't even call ol' boy a two-minute brotha. Barely a minute brotha, really. I have a new word for brothas like that: Nano Negro. That's just about how long it lasted—a nanosecond.

But guess what? Just when I thought he couldn't top his Nano Negro achievement, he did. As I pressed my hands against his sweaty, sticky chest to push him off I heard another deep, long, hog snort.

I shook my head. *I can't believe this.* This mofo fell asleep. On *top* of me!

I turned to the clock and saw 9:47. And it had *just* clicked to *that.* Wow.

This brotha done shot his load, then shot *himself* into a deep sleep. He had "parked" between my knees to get some ZZZs. Asshole.

As bad as I wanted him out, I didn't want to make the same mistake I did earlier and let that fool drive all drunk-e-fied. So I pushed him off me and nudged his body to the edge of the bed, until ... *ka-klunk!* He rolled smooth off the side.

Can you believe that fool still didn't wake up?

When I looked over the edge of the bed, I found him lying belly-down in front of my nightstand, face turned to the side—knocked the hell out! A coochie-induced coma did him in.

Somehow the condom had rolled off his toothpick onto my bed, staining my sheets with leftover drip. Ugh! Nasty! So you know what I did? I picked that thing up and dropped it on his pimpled butt—right on the crack. Yes, I did! And he *still* didn't wake up!

My buzz had slipped away, so I didn't even try to finish myself off. All them horny blood cells that had a sista fired up earlier shriveled up and went beddy-bye—just like Mr. Coochie Slaya from Da Himalayas lying on the carpet.

Yeah, I let him sleep it off. But by six in the morning? Girl, you'd better believe he caught a one-way ticket the hell out my comfort zone. And you know I decontaminated my bathroom with some Orange Action Lysol! Funky ass.

Oh, well. Bye, bye Lawrence. Enough of him.

Now, it couldn't have gotten any worse than that, right?

Chapter 4

Reject #3

Gene.

Cute *and* smart. Dame shame.

Met him at the African-American Cultural Fest in the San Diego Repertory Theatre. At that point, I was 'bout fed up with man-boys, but forced myself to keep it movin'. Post-Lawrence, I'd gone through a string of minute-and-a-half dates. You know, guy asks you out, you go to the movies, during the date he does something you don't like, and you step—never to be seen or heard from again. Not that it was a *complete* dry spell. I'll admit, I committed a couple of one-night hit-and-runs that I'm not too proud of. But I kinda thought Gene would end that long streak of never-wills.

Not to be, though. Gene didn't even get out the gate because I'm telling you, *that* fool definitely takes the cake out of every man I'd met before him and since!

Diane, a sista from the Human Resources department at my company, invited me to the festival. I'd seen a flier on her desk, commented that I wanted to go, and right then and there we made plans to do our thing together. Charlotte didn't roll with us 'cause she and Greg had reserved a cabin in Big Bear for a weekend getaway; no doubt trying to get the most out of Greg's baby juice supply.

At first glance, Gene looked like a nice, free-spirited, poetry-reading kinda brotha, sporting shoulder-length dreads that resembled the braids I still had. I noticed him among the thirty or so people in the Hip Hop session I attended, where we discussed the evolution of Hip Hop and current generation of rappers. It got heated at times, especially when we debated rap lyrics and use of the N-word. Gene had everybody's foreheads wrinkled up 'cause that fool had vocabulary for days. Shoot, I'd never heard the word "invidious" until I met him.

The intellectual Cornel West-type always turned me on, and homeboy definitely held my attention. Diane kept nudging me, whispering in my ear, talkin' 'bout, "he's looking at you, girl!" Yeah, I saw him. Caught him shining that easygoing smile my way a few times, and every time I saw him smiling, I would shoot one right back.

After several hours of workshops and speakers, the festival organizers moved the tables and chairs against the wall and pushed the stage curtains back to reveal a DJ standing over a pair of turntables. He spun an old LL Cool J record and within seconds, heads nodded. Guys and girls hooked up, booties bumped, and before you knew it, all that intense energy from the session dissolved into the positive vibe of an old-school house party.

Diane and I didn't play the wall too long. A buff brotha with a bald head and Todd Bridges face swept her onto the dance floor.

Gene stepped to me next. He asked, "Would you like to dance, sista?"

I nodded. Once we hit the floor, we embarked on a fantastic voyage back to the late 80's and early 90's.

We had one good-ass time, you hear me? The DJ rocked jams I hadn't heard since the Jheri curl days. Gene had me cracking up with dead-and-buried dances like the Roger Rabbit and the Smurf. Sweat drenched my face and arms 'cause I danced so hard. I was wavin' my hands in the air like I just didn't care.

Then the DJ slowed it down. I almost fell out when he bumped New Edition's "Can You Stand The Rain." I *love* that song!

Gene and I stayed on the floor, got our groove on, did the small talk thing. Of course, I checked him out. Damn cute. Cleft in his chin, bedroom eyes, toned build. Breath was a tad tart, but I forgave him for that 'cause we danced for an hour straight without drinking any water. Mine probably had that onion smell, too. A few breath mints took care of that, and eventually, cups of H20.

I had so much fun, dancing my spine out and stuff. The good time had to end, though.

After our two-hour journey back to the good old days, Diane, me, Gene, and Diane's Todd Bridges decided to call it a night. After they walked us to our car, Gene pulled out a brochure.

I checked it out. "The African American World History museum?"

"Yes, I was hoping we could experience it together."

Experience it, huh? "Well," I said, "I've never been to a black museum. Um ... that sounds fun. When?"

"Around noon tomorrow. I own a house off Market Street, so I'm five minutes away."

"You have a house, huh?"

He smiled. "Yeah, little teeny-tiny house, two bedroom. Figured we could meet up there and go in one car. It's hard to find parking in Old Town."

Little teeny-tiny house. Hmmm. A brotha with equity, it seemed. That impressed me. I definitely wanted to see how homeboy was livin'.

"Good idea," I said. "Sounds like a plan."

He smiled. I got directions to his house, we traded cell phone numbers, and that was that. I was looking forward to a laid-back afternoon with Gene, getting my cultural and educational juices flowing and what not. Man, was I wrong.

I parked in front of Gene's house. He had described it to a tee; it looked more like an oversized tree house than someone's residence. Really cute, though. It kinda had a turn of the century look.

Gene came running up from a cross street, huffing and puffing. It looked like he'd jogged halfway around San Diego and fell in the Pacific Ocean. Sweat drenched his white *Heart of San Diego Marathon* t-shirt and he wore a red and white bandana tied around his dreads.

Even though he told me to come by his house by 12:00—and it was 11:45—I didn't make a fuss 'cause he wasn't ready. I figured he'd shower, change clothes, slap on some Speed Stick, and we'd be out. I was thinking no more than twenty minutes.

Funny how you expect one thing and the opposite happens.

He took in a breath and smiled. "Hey."

I returned the smile. "Hi, Gene."

He went up the steps to his porch, fumbling around with his keys at the door. "Just finished a five-mile run. I thought I'd make it back before you got here."

Five miles, huh? I thought. *Not bad.* Shoot, I could barely run a mile without dry heaving. I love me a man who takes care of his body.

He inserted his house key. "You're looking beautiful."

A sista had to blush. First time a man called me the *other* B-word in I don't know how long. I wore a light blue blouse and jeans, nothing special. As long as I looked good to him, I was fine.

"Thank you," I said, smiling all hard, tugging on my braids and stuff.

Gene opened the door. Soon as I walked in a big whiff of underarm, feet, and ass funk rushed me. I was like, "Hel-lo!"

I stopped at the entrance. That smell had a sista's nose all seized up. Before I said anything, he said, "I had chitlins and pigs feet this morning." He walked over to a table and grabbed a can of air freshener. "I know most California folk aren't used to this smell. Sorry about that."

Damn right I wasn't used to that smell. He fumigated the living room with a heavy dose of Glade. Even though I have roots in Texas, chitlins and pigs feet just ain't my thing.

I walked toward the tan leather couch, holding my breath 'cause he sprayed so much it burned my eyes and stung my nostrils. "Uh ... stank ... I mean, *thank* you."

He placed the spray on the kitchen counter. "No problem. Make yourself at home. There's Apple juice in the fridge, glasses above the sink. Help yourself. I'm going to change."

"Okay. Thanks." I watched him disappear down a short hall.

After a minute or so, I got somewhat used to the funky fresh megamix, so I meandered around the room. Ran my hands over an African Congo mask on the wall, smiled at the itty-bitty dining table outside the kitchen, checked out the family pictures on a corner desk—you know, the usual nosy stuff. First and second-place trophies clogged a table underneath a dozen or so marathon awards stuck to the wall.

Didn't have much in the humble abode, but he had a nice place. Perfect for a bachelor, I guess. Despite the smell, he kept the joint spotless. Not bad for a single man.

I sat on the couch and grabbed an *Ebony* magazine from a nearby magazine rack.

I barely got through the first article before Gene reappeared talkin' 'bout, "You ready to go?"

When he came out, my eyebrows flew the hell up; my bottom lip fell the fuck down. He wore a beige sweater and dark-brown khaki pants, but that ain't what got me. What got me was how *fast* that fool came out. I was like, *hold up. I know this man didn't take a shower that quick. Did I even hear water running?*

I leaned back, gazing up at him while he tugged on the hem of his sweater, smoothing it out. I didn't know how to approach the situation 'cause I'd never been in it before. I was tongue-tied—a million wrinkles must've creased my forehead.

He broke my trance when he asked, "You all right?"

I shook my head, then blinked a few times. Somethin' damn sure wasn't right.

I had to say something, but didn't know where to start. "Dang, you ... uh ... take showers really fast. I didn't even hear the water running."

He chuckled. I didn't find anything funny, though.

Gene sat next to me and grabbed a bottle of lotion off the table. "You have something in your braids," he said.

That fool did *not* just sidestep my comment. I wasn't about to let it go 'cause the shit riled me up a bit, but I had to tend to the hair first. "Where?"

He leaned closer to me. While I tugged at my hair, he pulled a piece of lint out.

"I got it. Just some lint. It's no big thing."

Skkrrrr! I slammed on the brakes—*not* because of what he said. It was the renegades of funk that jetted out his mouth. His booty breath had pop-locked toward me, all up in a sista's grill. Made my eyelids flutter.

He had hardly said ten words when my nostrils suffered a knee-jerk reaction—just like when I first walked in the house. I'm talkin' breath so strong I swear if we were in a restaurant, the toxicity would contaminate the food.

While outside, I was too busy checking out his porch. Had I known about his breath then, I probably wouldn't have gone into the house. His tart breath was clearly an everyday thing and I'm sorry, Michelle can't handle a man with a nose-splittin' case of halitosis.

Still, I had to know what was up, so I went back to my shower comment. "Um ... you got one of those showerheads that don't make a lot of noise or somethin'? I was, uh, thinking about getting one." Such a lie.

He shifted his eyes from side to side, scratching his neck. "Oh, uh, I didn't take a shower. I just freshened up. It might seem different, but I'm one of those brothas who loves the intrinsic quality and olfactory beauty of human musk. Au naturale, if you will."

What?

Now, you know I laughed in that fool's face, right? Those fake-ass Harvard words didn't impress me, either. He could *not* have been serious, but he was! After I calmed down, I asked, "In other words you don't mind going outside funky?"

He smiled. "Well ... uh ... I guess you could put it like that."

I froze. I truly did not know how to respond. I mean, damn, how do you? He wasn't funky while we danced—even after dropping a gallon of sweat. Why was he funky now?

While dissecting his words, out of nowhere he said, "I usually bathe about three times a week. I just like to be in my ... uh"—he looked around, trying to find a good enough answer somewhere around that damn room, I guess— "my most natural, basic, human state. No soap, deodorant, toothpaste—nothing to taint my body. Most of those products are filled with harmful chemicals, you know."

It took me a few seconds to gather my senses. No shower? Are you kidding me? And this mofo had chitlins and pigs feet for *breakfast*, but he couldn't brush his teeth?

Oh *hells* no. I rubbed my nose, acting like it itched. "Gene?" I said. "Excuse me, but didn't you just run five miles? In the sun? When it's seventy-sum degrees out?"

Then I saw them, girl. Got a real good look. The one thing that makes me cringe the most: Jacked up teeth.

His teeth weren't chipped or criss-crossing at different angles like laser beams in a sci-fi movie—that wasn't the problem. No, I mean his teeth were littered with black dots. The *hell!* They looked fine in casual conversation, but when this fool threw back his head and busted up laughing for some reason, I peeked inside. Teeth looked like dice, girl. I kid you not. When he opened his mouth I thought I was looking at a craps table.

Lawd.

You remember those Saturday morning "Schoolhouse Rock!" cartoons from back in the day? Well, meet Yuck Mouth in the flesh. Who knew it was based on a real person?

He said, "I'm sorry, but you have this goofy look on your face!"

Homeboy held his belly like I said something hilarious. You woulda thought Cedric the Entertainer was up in the house. Then he continued, "It's okay, I swear! I showered yesterday and changed my shirt and shorts. I'm good to go."

What? I thought. *Showered yesterday? Changed my shirt and shorts?* Did he want a cookie for that? Damn it, what about ... his underwear? He did take the time to change those drawers, right?

Guess again.

I said, "You changed your shirt and shorts. That's it? You didn't change *anything* else?"

He still looked at me like he didn't understand. Steady rubbing lotion all up and down his arms. Wow. Don't need lotion if you ain't ashy. Can't be ashy unless you make contact with a heavy dose of water.

You know what he said? "Yeah, that's all I changed. I was just anxious to go. Are you ready?"

I dropped my head. *Lawd, why am I meeting all these rejects? Did he really just ask me if I was ready?*

Yeah, I was ready—ready for somebody to jump out the closet and yell, "Surprise!" This couldn't be real. It had to be an early April Fool's joke, a late Halloween prank ... something, right?

Nope, it wasn't. It was real—another man with issues. *Issshhhooos,* you hear me?

I didn't respond. I just turned my head away, mouth all open, thinking:

OK, let's recap: This grown ass man has stank breath; too many visits from the cavity creeps; cannot prioritize his showering cycle; said he didn't want to taint his body with deodorant or soap; and is wearing underwear that probably got fungus and fleas all up and down the crack of—

No! I couldn't do it. Hell no!

I don't care how nice a man is to me. He could bring me flowers, buy me diamonds, pay my bills—I don't give a damn. If you can't wash yo' own *ass?* Bruh! C'mon, now! You don't *need* to be all up in my area code.

I couldn't believe it. Just could not *believe* it.

That was it for me, girl. I saw the front of the door while that fool saw the back of my head. Since he couldn't understand good hygiene, a sista had to say "Goodbye, Gene."

After stepping outside into the fresh air—well, fresher than inside the house—I got in my car and zoomed away, leaving him on the porch, calling my name. I didn't want to hear it.

Never saw Gene again.

Still, I went to the museum by my damn self. Didn't call nobody to join me, just went. I'm funny like that sometimes. If a plan falls apart with someone, I'll just do whatever I was supposed to do by myself. No need to waste a trip somewhere when one person can't make it. In this case, I couldn't make it with this particular person. Gene had other priorities that needed immediate attention.

Got back to my empty abode, all by my lonesome. Now, don't get the wrong idea, I wasn't one of those sistas with tears on my pillow because the man fairy hadn't knocked on my door. I don't mind being alone, but I admit, sometimes having a man around is nice. So damn quiet in my one-bedroom apartment at times, too. I like filling the air with a perpetual flow of conversation and bed squeaks, ya know?

Shoot. Maybe I *was* getting lonely.

Hadn't had anything steady in a while. My last relationship lasted two years, but I broke that off some time ago. He's not even worth discussing. Let's just say the little head made most of his decisions. Punk ass.

I couldn't help rewinding images of the men I'd met recently. Damn, talk about cream of the "slop." An Anal Intruder, Mr. Thimble Dick, Captain Funkie Azz, damn! I mean, really, what is wrong with the male species? I couldn't believe my luck—or lack thereof. Was this really the dating pool I had to swim in? These were the city's most eligible bachelors? I was like "throw me a friggin' life raft 'cause I'm tired of floating around in this shit!"

I'd had enough. No more dumb ass men—at least for a little while.

Time to get my damn priorities straight, like school and working out. I'd been lollygagging about finishing my degree and slacking hard on my fitness. *Too* hard. The hardcore—uh, more like softcore— evidence of my jelly belly showed, too. Michelle was getting pudgy!

I patted the little pooch that used to be washboard. Damn shame. That last thing I needed was a gut. Used to go to my complex gym after my weak New Year's resolution, but stopped after a couple of weeks. I don't despise the gym; I'm just not a huge fan of it. But you gotta handle your bidness in order to maintain what ya got, ya know? And there I was, thirty-one years old pushing thirty-two, so maintaining an hourglass was going to be a lot harder.

I said, "Forget this. I'm getting my butt together."

I decided right then and there to do some major reconstruction. Not just for the health of my body, but for my mind as well.

So you know what I did? I set three goals: eat better, exercise more, and finish my Bachelors degree. I only had one semester left to get my piece of paper, but had put off those last few courses because ... hell, I don't know. Had a few issues with a school loan and kinda got burnt out on school, too. Then I was like "I only have one semester, so I'll get to it when I get to it." I guess I eventually convinced myself I was "too busy." Yeah, right. Not too busy to mess around with stupid men, though. Yup, my priorities were *all* jacked up.

That was it; I'd made up my mind. Men, clubbing, junk food—all that unnecessary clutter—got put on the backburner. I was ready for a project with guaranteed returns.

Time to focus on me, dag-nabbit. 'Bout time!

Chapter 5

Three months later

"How ya like me, now?" I said to homegirl in the mirror. I was ready for swimsuit season!

Checking myself out had become a daily thing since I committed to 24 Hour Fitness three months before. I'm not gonna lie—it was tough at first. Even though my apartment complex has a small gym, I figured the only way I'd stick to a workout regimen would be to pay for it. Hate seeing my dollars go to waste, so a sista psyched herself up, got some new gear, filled up the iPOD with new jams, and got all Donna Richardson up in that place.

And it paid off 'cause my body was firm, tight, and sex-a-licious. I would even say I'd become Serena Williams-like.

Well ... not quite. That's pushing it, but dammit, I was on my sexy way.

I felt pretty damn proud of myself. For too many months, I'd wasted time on mess that didn't pay dividends for me, mostly on men—but not much of anything for *Michelle*. Well, I'm happy to report I finally got my priorities in order—it's all about Michelle's future and health. Sometimes, women have to do that. We need to say, "Bump everybody else. I'm doing some things for my damn self to make *me* happy."

I'd traded my Burger King, Taco Bell and Popeyes eating plan for homemade salads, protein shakes, lean meats, and fruits. Hit the gym after work every Monday, Wednesday and Friday—the same days as my classes. That worked out just fine. After my workouts, I'd shower, dress, and by six o'clock, get a three-hour dose of edumucation.

I got down and got it *done!* Did everything I said I would do within a three-month window. And wouldn't you know it? Last time I stood on the scale I was twenty pounds lighter! Not only that, I finished my classes! I could finally see myself in a black gown with degree in hand.

I think I can brush my shoulders off now.

One day at work, Charlotte called to ask if I could escape for fifteen minutes 'cause she wanted to talk about something important. I was due for a break anyway, so I told my supervisor, Ms. Cawlings, I was stepping out for a little while. Charlotte and I agreed to meet in the lobby. After my three-floor descent down the stairs—no more elevators—I scanned the lobby for Charlotte. This scraggly FedEx man was walking my way with a package in hand when he damn near tripped over his lips as his jaw hit the floor. His quick pace stutter-stepped almost to a halt.

Of course, I knew where his sudden trance came from. I had my new hourglass on blast again in a gold V-neck tee and dark-brown mini skirt. Just like all the other fellas that peeped when I walked by, I turned and caught him checking out my legs, too. Since I toned everything up, I'd seen more twinkles in mens' eyes than I could count. These fools weren't subtle at all, each one looking like they wanted to throw me to the ground and booty-smack me like a damn paddle. Nasty freak-a-zoids.

Charlotte stood from her chair. "Damn, girl. You see how hard that fool was staring at you?"

I huffed. "Don't pay that man no mind. He's a horny ass dog. He can't help it."

She wrapped her purse around her shoulder. "Yeah, but damn. It looked like he wanted to chew off your clothes and slobber you down."

I pushed the glass door and stepped outside. "Like I said—a dog. Ruff, ruff." Charlotte laughed.

We walked to the small courtyard beside the building and found an empty bench. As we sat down, Charlotte said, "You're not going to believe what I saw on HBO last night."

I took a sip from my bottled water. "Fool, is this what you pulled me out of work to tell me?"

She banged her fist on the carved stone table. "Just listen girl, damn!"

I played along. "All right, what did you see?"

"Thank you!" She rolled her eyes. "Anyway, Greg fell asleep with the TV on, and when I woke up in the middle of the night, there was this old, crusty, bushman on the TV standing in front of a pail of water with a stick in his hand."

I frowned. Had no idea where she was going with her Bushman story, so I just nodded.

She said, "I found the remote and was about to turn the TV off when I noticed him wrapping this bamboo-lookin' stick around the pail handle."

I took another sip. "And why was he doing that?"

She smiled. "It wasn't a stick, girl. Well ... in a way, it was."

She turned and swerved her head around, looking for God knows what. I did the same thing, wondering if I missed something. Nobody stood within earshot of our conversation. Just a couple of joggers in the distance running the dirt trails that circled our building.

I turned to her. "Well, what was it?"

She leaned toward me, cuffed a hand over her lips and dropped her voice to a whisper. "*It was his thing.*"

I threw my head back. "What?"

"I'm not lying, girl," she said, struggling to hold back chuckles. "I swear this thing was as long as my leg. I was like, 'what the hell am I watching?' Then I noticed it was HBO. Probably *Real Sex* or something."

"Hold up, hold up!" I cried, waving my hands, getting all loud and ghetto. "That man used his—"

"Shhhhh!" Charlotte said, pressing her finger to her lips.

I lowered my voice. "That man picked up a pail of water with his *dingaling*? How the hell did he do that?"

"Used it like a rope. He bent down, pulled the handle up, got his thing under it, held the head with his other hand—and picked that bucket up, girl! I almost fell out!"

I damn near choked I laughed so hard. "Girrrrl, how long was it?"

She spread her hands apart. "Narrator said something about it being a little over *thirteen inches!* Not quite fourteen, but damn, that's big enough! The narrator said he had one of the longest ding-dongs in the world. Can you believe that?"

My jaw dropped. "Daaaaayum! And he was using that thing to pick up buckets? Talk about a waste of talent! Shoot, I need to find *me* a Sir Dick-a-Lot like that!"

We let ourselves go—clapping, high-fiving, screaming, damn near falling off our seats. I laughed so hard my eyes rained.

As we calmed down, an image of a man with a bat for a penis flashed inside my head. The mental picture chilled me. Couldn't imagine what I'd do if I met a man with superhuman penile power. Most women don't get so lucky.

I wiped my wet cheeks. "That is too funny. Damn. Can you see Greg with a thing that long?"

"Hell yeah!" Charlotte cried. Shocked me that she responded so fast.

Her voice got low again. She said, "I *wish* Greg was hung like that. I'd probably be so happy with that thing I'd take snapshots and hang them in my cubicle. Have people coming by my desk, staring at all my pictures. I'd be pointing and stuff, talking about 'this is me on my honeymoon, my dog Winston, and oh—my husband's dick.' "

We *rolled*. I thought my sides would split open.

Charlotte wiped her cheeks with a tissue from her purse. "Wooo, girl. Imagine the possibilities."

Imagine the possibilities. I repeated those words in my head. Never experienced a "King Dingaling" before. Don't think any of my friends have, either.

I tucked that fantasy away in a corner of my mind. The odds of me finding a man like that were about the same as me hitting the California jackpot with one set of lottery numbers. Impossible.

"Michelle?" Charlotte said, breaking my trance. "Damn, girl, you grinning like you just had an orgasm or something. Speaking of which, when was the last time you got some?"

That comment dented my mood and slammed me back into my man-less world. "All right, girl. I don't want to hear it."

"Hear what? That you've been dissin' brothas left and right? I don't know how many times some guy has come by my desk trying to get your phone number from me. I'm like 'dang, ask *her* for it!' "

I shrugged. "I know, I know. I have guys trying to drop lines on the job all the time. I'm just not feelin' anybody right now."

"Nobody's feeling *you*, either."

I chuckled, but the truth stung a bit. Three months without any nookie and my coochie had cobwebs.

"You miss your ex at all?"

My smile turned upside down. Now, why she gotta go and bring up my ex?

"Hell, no! Sorry, cheatin' asshole." Charlotte laughed.

But, I'd lied just a little. The ex could damn near make me claw up the walls with his tongue action and penile wizardry. He popped in my head and I held back chills. At that moment, a one-night stand with him sounded like just what the doctor ordered.

As my mind drifted away, I noticed Charlotte gazing at me.

I said, "Ho, why are you staring so hard?"

She twisted her lips. "You're not trying to come out the closet, are you?"

Her question made me whip my head to the left. Where in the world did that come from? "What? Girl, be quiet. You know Michelle is strictly dickly. Don't even try it."

But as I thought about my recent dry spell, I realized I'd been putting out some kind of man-repellant vibe. I'd been so focused on my goals and finishing school that I'd gotten used to not giving men the time of day—in the gym, at work, at school, on the street.

I didn't want anybody trying to holla at me and mess up a sista's flow, ya know? Men tend to do that.

But I had no good reason to play hard-to-get anymore. Why not let my guard down a little?

I wanted to get off that subject, so I asked, "Are you going to tell me what you *really* wanted to talk about?"

A long sigh breezed through her lips. "Oh, I don't know." She paused, tapped her fingers, looked around, then took in a deep breath. "Just wondering what to name your play niece."

My bottom lip dropped. "What? No!"

She smiled and nodded like one of them bobble head dolls. I jumped up so fast I banged my knee against the table. Damn, it hurt. Felt like I cracked my kneecap, but I sucked it up and hobbled over to my homegirl-mommy-to-be.

"Damn girl, you all right?" she asked.

I didn't respond—just grabbed her hands, pulled her up, then smothered her. "Congratulations!" I cried. "Shh-ow."

"Thank you."

"Wow!" I said. I sat back down and faced her. After wiping away stone residue from my knee, I stroked it. "I'm finally gonna be an auntie, huh?"

"Yes, lawd!" she cried. "Took us a while, but one of Greg's little soldiers finally hit the target."

I shook my head, trying to take it all in. Couldn't believe it. My girl officially had a new role now; one that required a lot of give-and-take.

"Dang," I said, "I'm all finished with school, summer's 'bout to start and I'm ready to go clubbin' again! But you wind up pregnant? How dare you?"

"Hey, don't blame me," Charlotte said, waving her hand. "Blame the guy who kept sticking his thing in me every night."

"Ewww! I didn't need to hear all that!"

We laughed, slappin' hands, carryin' on like best friends do. But I knew the moment she revealed the baby news, I wouldn't see her as much, at least not outside of work. We had entered a new era of Lamaze classes, crib shopping, umpteen doctor visits. Geez. Part of me felt sad, knowing things between us would never be quite the same.

On top of that, she had a man to take care of her needs. And I mean, *all* of them. Including someone to stick a "thing" in her every night.

I decided to loosen my man-guard that day.

Time to test the waters again—but with a better screening process. I didn't want a man with issues. *Issshhhooos*, ya know?

Funny how fate plays jokes on a sista.

Chapter 6

June in San Diego is like one big oven set on "bake." The moment you step outside sweat bursts through your pores and shit. Most people stay inside, unless at the beach or in the pool. The heat was fine with me, though. It motivated a sista that much more to get into the cool air-conditioned gym.

I stepped out of the apartment on Saturday morning around nine. Before I left for the gym, I'd been yapping it up on the phone with Charlotte. She told me she and Greg were looking into Lamaze classes and reading up on baby stuff.

Man. So weird, ya know? Still couldn't get over the news. No more clubbing with her for at least a year.

I headed for my car, carrying a bottle of Gatorade with my San Antonio Spurs towel around my neck. Had my tight body on display, too, wearing a cute navy and red sports bra with matching tights. The spandex hugged my twins and Beyoncé booty. Topped off my sexy attire with a pair of aqua-colored shades, looking oh-so fine, I must say.

As I skipped down the last flight of stairs, I saw this cut brotha walking up the metal ramp of a medium-sized U-Haul truck. Looked like he was moving into the apartment building across from mine.

He disappeared for a few seconds, then emerged carrying a Plasma TV. It must have been at least forty inches, but he made carrying it seem effortless.

Brothaman kinda strong, I thought. I even nibbled my lip 'cause the image of him working up a sweat looked pretty damn tasty. I love that sweaty, dirty, men-at-work look.

Being the nosy somebody that I am, you know I had to pull a CSI and investigate. I strutted toward him, ready to get my fill of eye-candy. At first, I didn't get a good look at him because a baseball cap half-covered his face, but he wore the hell out of that white tank top, so I took note of his chest and arms. The thin layer of sweat made those thick, well-toned bad boys glisten like Kobe Bryant after forty five minutes on the court. A sista was like *dayum!*

He stepped off the ramp and set the TV in the small patch of grass next to the sidewalk. I was thinking, *I hope he's not a moving guy. Why brothas always got to be the hired help? This place could definitely use some extra chocolate up in here, especially if they look like him.*

You know I stared at that booty, too. Couldn't see a good outline 'cause of the baggy gray sweatpants and long tank top. Oh well.

I was a few feet away when he stood and stretched his back, so I slowed my pace. As he turned in my direction, he took off his cap and wiped the sweat from his clean-shaven head with his shirt. I caught a glimpse of sculpted abs. Bald head and a six-pack. Like cherries in an Apple Martini. Nice combination.

Double dayum, I thought.

When I finally got a good look at him, I slammed on my imaginary brakes. Entranced, enraptured, enchanted—whatever you wanna call it—I felt it. That fool was F-to-the-I-N-E *fine*, you hear me? I'm talking dark-brown skin, Morris Chestnut lips, baller height. Yummy. He looked like a brotha straight out of an Arabesque romance novel, except I wasn't turning the pages in some book, salivating over an exaggerated fantasy. Oh no. The black Mr. Clean stood right before me.

Our stares locked for a few seconds. We stood like two fools unable to use our lips. Our initial reaction got somewhat comical after a while, considering how long we stared, our eyes traveling up and down, absorbing the image of each other like two hungry people standing before a triple cheeseburger. My breastesses poking out of the sports bra held his eyes on lockdown longer than what's appropriate. But I didn't really mind 'cause I was caught up in my own inappropriate eye-ballin'.

My heartbeat triple-timed while this man towered over me. I even had to tilt my neck back a little. That fool stood at least six four, head touching the clouds and shit.

I took my sunglasses off. "Heavy TV, huh?"

Damn. Soon as I said that, I wanted to shove my *own* foot up my ass. So corny.

He put the cap back on his head, backwards this time. "Uh, yeah."

My eyebrows shot up. The thunder in his voice caught me off guard. Homeboy had that bass thing going. The deeper the voice, the weaker my knees get. Lawd.

"I only have that lamp left," he said, pointing to the back of the truck. "Do you, uh, mind getting it for me?"

"Oh!" I said, sounding all surprised. I turned and saw an iron lamp with antique finish. Pretty nice. It seemed he had good taste.

"I don't mind," I said. "I'll get it."

I trotted my butt up the ramp, grabbed the lamp, and then embarked on my little journey with Chocolate Thunder.

After he picked the TV back up, homeboy climbed the steps like he wasn't even carrying anything. *Fine and obviously in shape. Check one and two.*

We reached the second floor. His apartment was the first one at the top of the stairs, the door already open.

Building four, apartment 215 ... building four, apartment 215. Why I repeated his apartment number in my head, I have no idea. Guess I wanted to make sure I could find my way back—*if* I came back, of course. Ain't like my goofy butt could forget, though. He lived like two seconds away.

I followed him inside. He had the same model as mine—the 900-square foot one-bedroom with wide-open kitchen, which told me he picked it so he could get his chef groove going. That's why I chose mine.

Hmmm, I thought, *he must be a good cook. I can see him whippin' up a nice little dish for me.*

He placed the TV on a black stand. "Well, this is my spot, the last one in this model. Got it 'cause of the big kitchen. A brotha loves to cook."

Ha! I knew it! Check three!

I wanted to clap for some reason. I said, "I know what you mean. I love to cook, too."

We smiled and stared. Flutters tickled my insides. I really felt like I was back in junior high when I had a crush on my Phys Ed teacher, Mr. Burlson. He was the finest man ever.

Well, let me amend that. Mr. Burlson's second now. Mr. Mystery Man had just stolen the top spot.

I cleared my throat. "This lamp staying in the living room?"

"Yeah, go 'head and set it by the couch, please."

I took a quick survey of the room. My gaze bounced all around, searching for anything female-related—floral prints, happy-couple pictures, pretty little plants, high-heeled shoes—that kind of stuff. I didn't see anything.

For a second, I even had an itch to conduct the female inspection —you know, that can-I-use-your-bathroom-so-I-can-rummage-around-in-your-cabinets trick. Almost did it, girl, but I blew away that nonsense.

Other than a few boxes with labels like "glass" and "bedroom," it looked like he had everything pretty much set up. Nice leather sofa behind a square glass coffee table with pine surrounding the glass. Afrocentric paintings of a jazz ensemble with that Cotton Club feel propped against the far wall. A Mac computer with a large monitor sat on a corner desk next to the couch.

Brothaman had style.

I really hope a woman didn't have something to do with this, except maybe his mother, I said in my head.

I set the lamp beside the couch, next to an open box marked "books." I peeked inside and saw a book titled *Think and Grow Rich: A Black Man's Choice.*

Hmmm, I thought, *he's a reader, too. Dang, check four.*

Since we hadn't really spoken much on the way up—other than small talk about him moving most of his stuff by himself 'cause his friend couldn't make it—I started yapping.

Looking up at him, I said, "I see you like to read, huh?"

He raised and folded his arms, his fists balled, stretching his back out with a side-to-side rotation. I saw the cuts in his muscles and swallowed—hard.

"I love to read," he said, grunting. "Especially black fiction, believe it or not. I probably read more than I watch TV. I try to read a new black author every month."

Wow, I thought, nodding. *Not bad. Not bad at all.*

"I read about three books a month myself," I replied. "Got everything stored on my Kindle. I'm always curled up in bed at night with a good read."

Damn. Blabbermouth, huh? I had gone straight to the bedroom secrets, and I hadn't known the man more than five minutes. Shoot, I didn't even know his name yet. Another bad habit—talking too damn much and exposing private info too damn soon.

"No doubt," he said. He walked up to me. My heart tried to pry a hole through my chest. I got all hot in the face as the distance between us grew smaller. "Thank you for bringing my lamp. I'm Daryl, by the way. I would shake your hand, but I'm pretty sweaty."

Damn, that voice. Soothed my soul like the sound of a waterfall.

I raised my hand anyway. "That's all right. A little sweat never hurt anyone," I said with a wink. He wiped his hand on his shirt and enveloped my hand. I still felt some sweat, but dag-nabbit, I didn't care. I just wanted to touch him and merge his natural moisture into mine.

"I'm Michelle. It's nice to meet you."

Again, our glances attached. Again, I swallowed.

I really hope he's feelin' me like I'm feelin' him, I thought.

I'm pretty sure he liked what he saw since I wore an outfit that exposed all my delectable edibles. Then again, a woman could look like the Elephant Man and still have a man's tongue wagging—as long as she had an ass. And I had ass for *days*.

Schoolyard-crush vibes rushed through my veins, the kind where you gotta focus on every word that comes out of your mouth to stifle dumb ass remarks. I already had one "X" in the box for saying something silly earlier.

A moment passed before he said, "So ... uh ... you're going to the gym, huh? Cool. That's one of the reasons why I moved here."

I acted surprised. "Really? Well, I can confirm the complex gym is nice. I used to work out all the time but haven't been in a while because I don't have a partner."

I did it again—exposed more secret info. At the rate I was going I probably would have revealed my bra size next. Words rolled out of my mouth like I didn't have control of my tongue.

"I try to go as much as I can," he said. "I would go today, but I have to take the truck back and set up my apartment."

Damn. For some reason it didn't dawn on me that this man had more important things to do. I guess I thought he would drop all his business, scoot on down to the gym with me, and be at my beck and call. I must've sounded desperate.

I was just about to backpedal when he added, "But, I'll definitely check it out tomorrow. I should be finished unpacking by then. You go on Sundays, too?"

Hell no, I thought. I usually didn't work out on Sundays, but best believe I was fixin' to make an exception.

"Uh ... yeah. I usually do the ... um ... treadmill on Saturday and dumbbells on Sunday."

I was proud of myself for getting through that lie with a straight face. I never saw any parts of the gym on Sundays, but if this was my only chance to see him again, I was down like four flat tires.

"Cool," he replied. "You go there around this time?"

"Um ... usually around ten. I like to sleep in on Sundays."

"All right, then. I'll definitely check you out tomorrow."

That was my cue to let him get back to his business. Although giddy inside, I played it cool and said, "Good. Can't wait. Well, I'll get out of your way and let you do your thing."

Before I made a move, Daryl walked to the doorway. "I'll walk you down. I gotta close up the truck and get it back anyway."

He let me walk past him while standing in the doorway. Yup, had that look, too. You know what I'm talkin' 'bout. He wasn't even slick. Homeboy wanted to check me out while I walked down the steps. Typical male.

I wasn't mad, though. I *wanted* him to check out the results of all those damn lunges, leg lifts and butt raises I'd been doing for the last few months. Somebody should be appreciatin' all my hard work!

When we reached the bottom of the stairs, I turned, waved, and gave him a big smile before heading toward the gym. Of course I had my schemin' hat on. I trotted along, wiggling the jelly like ol' girl in *Waiting to Exhale*.

As I turned the corner, I saw him still standing in the same spot. That famished daze in his eyes told me he wanted to slop my booty up in a biscuit and tear it up, girl!

You know what? I really think the wiggle worked.

Chapter 7

We started vertical, Daryl's face inches from the aura of desire that blazed through my body. Daryl leaned closer, then positioned the full weight of steel in front of me.

I inhaled, capturing the fresh minty flavors of his breath inside my lungs. Careful. Slow. Up, then down. Up, then down. His large, dark hands grazed my forearms, then my elbows. I continued my motion, elevating until my muscles contracted. Gritting my teeth, I tried to summon more strength, but I had reached my peak and couldn't take any more.

"There you go," he said. "You got it."

And I didn't think I'd like curl-ups.

Daryl watched me complete fifteen repetitions with ten-pound weights on the curl bar. He'd placed his hands under my arms, poised to rescue me if my strength gave way.

Lawd, lawd, lawd.

Just talking about his chocolaty presence stirs warmth within me like a glass of Riesling.

Daryl counted during my reps, his deep voice resonating through my ears, firing tingles along my spine that detonated inside my inner thighs. I am not lyin', the brotha had me gripped. His aftershave would yank my nostril hairs and it took all my strength to keep from running my nose up and down his neck. I sucked in a big glob of air, merged that sweet fragrance into me, then placed the bar on the floor.

"Woooo," I said while shaking my arms out, "you trying to work a sista, huh?"

He walked around the bench and grabbed two thirty-five pound weights. His plump lips rose into a grin. "You did just fine on your own. You can work me out, now."

Damn, that sounded good.

He handed me a weight. We both bent down and placed the weights on the bar, stealing glances and adolescent smiles at each other. I was still catching my breath from my reps, but when he stood and started curling? *Girl!* An earthquake could've erupted around us and I *still* wouldn't have noticed. Can't tell you how much watching him turned me on.

Up.

Down.

Up.

Down.

I had to do it, girl. I had to pull more sneak moves. When he'd lower the bar, his knuckles would pass my breasts by inches. I couldn't miss my chance. I sidestepped a little to my left. His knuckles dropped again. I closed my eyes, for just a second.

And he touched them.

Okay, I admit he only brushed me, but I almost became one with the floor when he did 'cause I swear I lost blood flow in my knees for a hot second.

I know, I know. I'm so damn silly, huh?

"You're going to help me when I can't lift any more, right?" he asked.

I broke from my freaky-deaky trance. I *wanted* to say, "Oh, I can help you 'lift', all right." But I played good girl and said, "Of course, Daryl. Anything to help maintain that hard body of yours." He smiled.

Oh! Speaking of that body.

Damn ... that body.

Toned.

Tall.

Tasty.

My three favorite "T's."

He wore a flimsy sleeveless shirt, so I had an unobstructed view of his arms at work. Wooo! Damn, I love me some nice biceps, too. Like two large, Grade A pieces of USDA prime trimmed of all fat. And right before my eyes, they went up ... down ... up ... down. Lawd.

Made me wonder about another kind of "meat" I wouldn't mind seeing in the same rhythm, ya know?

I dropped my eyes toward his southern region, stealing peeps here and there to spur my imagination. No go. The tail of his long-ass shirt and baggy sweats concealed his prized possession.

Dag-nabbit.

He was still raising the bar, concentrating hard on his reps. Me? I was too busy concentrating on *him*. Shoot, I think after four reps, I lost count. That fool had my mind wrapped around his biceps.

As he lifted, he grunted several times. Those gritty, throaty sounds made my mind stray off to another kind of physical activity I could see myself getting into with him.

Hmmm, I thought, *he sounds sexy when he makes those noises. I wonder if he sounds like that when he's having an orga—*

"...asms. Big time. Man, they were intense."

My eyebrow curled up as I broke free from another Daryl-induced daze. I was like, *hold up, what did he say? I know he didn't just say what I think he said.* I know I'd been fading in and out, but I wasn't *that* far gone.

I cleared my throat. "Um, what was that?"

The bar tapped his chest. "I said, after doing curl-ups I used to have back spasms. I don't have them ... *ugh* ... anymore. Help me out, please."

Ooooh. Back spasms.

I helped him raise the bar for one last rep. When he set the weights down, he shook out his arms and set his hands on his hips. I kinda stared at him for a second. Didn't see or hear anything else—except him. He must have noticed me gawking 'cause he flashed me a bright smile.

I gathered my senses. *All right, Chelle. Let's get it together now. Stop staring at this man.*

He stepped over to the exercise bench. "So," he said, "you wanna work on shoulders, now?"

I blinked away my thoughts. "Um ... sure."

I had just picked up the weights when he said, "Aw hell. Another one."

My eyebrows shot up. "Another what?"

"Another San Antonio fan. I just noticed your towel. You know they ain't going to win the championship this time, right? Lebron and the Heat are gonna take it this year."

Oh, I didn't like that. He did *not* just diss my Spurs. Soon as he said that, I was no longer a starry-eyed ball of lust trying to figure out what to say. I had to let him know he couldn't hate on my team.

The weights tapped each other over my head. "Boy, are you crazy? Miami is not going to win a damn thing! You know we gonna take it this year! Game three is tonight and they about to spank that ass. Don't hate, now."

He cracked up. "Don't hate, huh? We'll see who's hatin' tonight."

I tilted my head toward Daryl and said, "Yeah, okay. Somebody's 'bout to get spanked tonight. Watch. "

He laughed. It surprised him how much I knew about pro basketball. We yapped on like two chatterboxes with broken "Mute" buttons. We went back and forth: him swearing up and down Dwayne Wade and Lebron would do this and that; me reminding him that Duncan and my future baby-daddy Tony Parker weren't tryin' to hear that. When it comes to the NBA, a sista can hang with the best of them.

After the weights, we hit the exercise bikes. Conversation carried over from sports to personal stuff. It's funny how at first my triple-X mind peeled away his clothes, but once we got to talking, it was all innocent. I hadn't had an intelligent conversation with a man in a long time. And you know what? It felt good.

We got into each other's business about almost everything—work, school, future plans, his volunteer work mentoring kids—just on and on. I loved the way he gestured with those huge hands, too, even while riding the bikes. I just knew he could do some damage with those things. And I'm not talkin' 'bout the destructive kind of damage, either.

Got to a point where I forgot I was working out. What drew me in most was that he was clearly a "man in transition," as he put it. You know, the I-don't-wanna-be-a-playa-no-more type. Apparently going to clubs every weekend and picking up chickenheads bored him. Said he got tired of all the hit-it-and-quit-it moments and was ready to slow it down. Oh yeah, he got real on a sista.

I told him I recently had a similar epiphany. We agreed that certain things got old after a while, and reevaluating one's priorities became necessary as you got older. Talk about coincidence—we had all kinds of stuff in common.

It surprised me how well he expressed himself. Just talkin' 'bout everything. Wow, a man who can break down his true feelings? Believe it or not, girlfriend, they *do* exist.

It got to a point where he was blabbering more than me, opening himself up like a busted piñata. I didn't know another person existed that could outdo my motor mouth. I ate it all up, too. I figured since he wanted to settle down and was revealing so much, he must've seen me as a potential settle-down partner. Girl, the man basically threw me a line and hook, so I made my eye contact, smiled a lot, and listened to everything he said 'cause you know what? I was a fish ready to bite.

We stayed in that gym for another hour after we finished working out, just blabbing away. We got comfortable, sitting on two benches, just goin' on and on. The only reason we stopped is because this Barry Manilow lookin' guy and a Barbara Bush clone walked in. Two was cozy, but four? Definitely a crowd.

While taking slow baby steps toward our respective apartments, Daryl said, "I've never done that before."

"Done what?" I replied.

He shrugged. "I've never stopped working out then laid up in the gym just talking to somebody." He looked down at me, big ol' grin on his face. Tingles raced through me.

"Yes, that was nice," I said. "Now that we live about two seconds from each other I guess we can talk all we want, huh?"

"Yup. I guess we can."

I smiled *hard.* Probably looked like the Joker from Batman with my lips curled up.

We turned the corner of his building. I had my fingers knotted up, damn near dislocating my joints. Hands so damn clammy it felt like my palms were underwater. Crazy how when you're cravin' a man so much it can throw your bodily functions all outta whack. I sucked in some air, then checked my watch.

"Wow," I said, to break a short moment of silence, "it's damn near one o'clock. We were in there a while, huh?"

"Yeah." He stopped in front of the stairs to his apartment. While gritting his teeth, he said, "I had a good time, too, though I'm probably gonna be sore. The way you worked a brotha, my whole body hurts."

I chuckled. "Shoot, I'm gonna be the one all sore and stuff. I'll probably need one of those deep tissue massages before I go to bed."

Damn! I dropped hints harder than bombs over Baghdad. I probably should've thought before I spoke, but those hands ... damn. Warped my mind, burning a tasty image in my head. I could feel those bad boys on me, caressing my soft skin ... his hard fingers deep-stroking the curves on my baby-oiled body ... massaging my ... wooo!

I need to stop!

We stood tongue-tied for a few seconds. Then he broke the silence when he said, "Kinda funny how after an hour of sharing my life story, I don't know what to say right now."

Ain't that the truth. I was feeling the same damn way.

My heart acted the fool, thumping so fast it almost had a techno beat to it. I said, "Yeah, I know ejactly ... *exactly* what I ... you mean."

Ugh! Just stuttering like a fool! Damn! So embarrassing! I felt my face flush.

He chuckled. "Yeah. So, Ms. Larsen, you busy tonight?"

I scratched my thigh, but locked my gaze on him. "Uh, no plans. What do you have in mind?"

"I'd like to cook for you and maybe make it a Netflix night," he said. "I have a coupla DVDs that I haven't watched yet."

I played it cool. The best I could, of course. "That would be nice I wanted to see what you could do what time?"

So much for being cool. I meant to say three different sentences, but it came out so fast I'd jumbled them all into *one* sentence. Ugh! It made him chuckle, though. A sexy, deep kind of giggle that seemed to come from the pit of his stomach. It accentuated those plump lips; lips that rose into a smile that sparked ripples through me.

Lips I wanted him to test-drive around the soft region between my thighs.

Lips I could test tonight.

"How about six?" he said.

Didn't really matter to me what movies he had. Shoot, as long as Daryl was next to me on the couch we could watch *Muppets Go to Mars* and it would have been fine with me.

I said, "Sounds good."

He slapped his hands together and smirked like what I said made his day. "Cool. Well, I'm gonna get on outta here. Gotta shower and hit the grocery store."

Lawd. I could see a steady stream of hot, steamy water splashing against his buffet of pecs, abs, arms, and "hard hot link" on the side. I shook away that image 'cause I didn't want to wet myself.

"Um, yeah," I said, still recovering. "Let me know if you need me to bring anything."

"The only thing I need is for you to be at my front door by six o'clock."

Pretty smooth, huh? That comment stapled a grin on me. Gotta admit when he said that I jellied up, got all cozy and warm inside.

"Well, I'll see you tonight," he said. "Thanks for helping a brotha maintain this body."

"Thank you for helping me with *this* body," I said. "But, in order to maintain it, I need to keep this up. I hope we can do it again."

He walked up the steps. "Oh, no doubt. We can talk about it later, maybe set up a schedule. We'll work it out tonight, so don't be late."

"Work it out tonight," the man said. Good Lawd. Daryl had no idea how bad I wanted to get "worked." He could press his weight on me any time.

I waved at him then pretty much floated back to my apartment. Before I flooded my mind with "what am I going to wear?" questions, you know the first thing I did when I got inside? You got it. I went straight to the bedroom, stripped off the white bed linen and replaced them with my purple and black silky satin sheets and comforter set. A sista had to be prepared!

While showering, tingles raked through my torso and inner thighs. Daryl lit up in my head like Japanese fireworks. I had to keep myself from performing a few solo acts, ya know? I stood under the water, just singin' and carryin' on, actin' the fool. So silly of me, as always. I was over-the-top chipper, Mr. Rogers-on-speed goofy.

But you know what? I didn't care.

The way I saw it, forget trying to fight the feeling 'cause I wanted to see Daryl's chocolate ass decked on my bed ten seconds after we met. Just gotta keep it real. I had no idea what he would cook, but whatever the dish, it damn sure wouldn't compare to the hormonal blaze that Daryl and three months of celibacy had ignited in me.

Time to put an end to that streak. I'd become the Sahara Desert in need of steady moisture, and damn it, I was fixin' to make Daryl my oasis.

Chapter 8

I have all these clothes but a sista can't find a thing! I could wear those jeans, but they make my butt look big. But, then again, it's my best asset—I want him to see my butt. What I really need to decide is if I should wear something sexy, or go casual, or...

"Damn!" I screamed. I was standing in the middle of my bedroom in my bathrobe, words whirling around in my head faster than an ice skater's spin moves. Nerves actin' buck-wild, closet all jacked up. It was crazy; *I* was crazy. Just yanking clothes off the hangers. Pants, skirts, blouses spread out all over the damn place. You woulda thought I'd won a one-minute shopping spree at Macy's.

Get your ass together, Michelle!

Guess I was on autopilot. I don't friggin' know. I really had to remind myself that I was just going to the man's apartment. Can you believe I thought about slithering into a mini-skirt with no panties?

Yup. I know—acting the fool. But 'cha know what? It felt good. All that outta whack energy had shifted my motor skills into 5th gear. The jitters, the butterflies, my thumpity-thump heartbeat—all because I wanted to leave a mental mark on a fine-ass man. I really felt like I might have found my prince among frogs.

However, I couldn't let him know how *much* I longed to lick the sweat off his back, ya know? I couldn't come off *too* desperate and shit. Didn't matter that I was aching to get freak-nasty like a pair of rabbits; what mattered was my need for *him* to make the first move. After that, I would just let nature do its thang. Of course, I would risk looking easy, considering I hadn't known the man more than forty-eight hours. But dag-nabbit, I was willing to take that risk. I'd let the sway in my hips, the thick muscles in my thighs, the lump of my rump, and the curve in my breasts talk for me, more than my lips could ever do.

When Daryl and I had our rap session in the gym, I think my lovable, playful yet intellectual side attracted him. And it didn't hurt that I love sports, too, especially basketball. Men like women who know the difference between a power forward and a tight end.

Speaking of tight ends, you *know* he X-rayed my lovely lady lumps and everything else I got goin' on, too. The magnetic pull of a black woman's brick house can seize a man's mind better than the world's greatest hypnotist! Make them do all kinds of crazy stuff, all because of a bangin' boo-tay.

Anyway, after spending too damn long trying on different outfits, I realized I just had to be myself. I got my bearings and rifled through my clothes one last time. As I picked through blouses, skirts and pants, I noticed the smooth touch of my legs blessing the full-length mirror. Loved the results of three dedicated months to my fitness routine—and it showed. With a smile and nod, I came to one conclusion:

"Damn, I'm sexy!"

I tell ya, girl, you might think I'm crazy but when I saw my fine ass in the mirror, I wanted to screw my damn self! I am not lyin'! Nothing pleases a woman more than a nice figure in the mirror.

After I broke from my "I'm too sexy" trance, I looked at the nightstand clock and noticed it was 5:30. Kicking it up a notch, I pulled a silk bra from the top drawer of my dresser and strapped it on. Deciding to roll with a casual yet sexy look, I grabbed a white blouse from the mountain of clothes on the bed and ironed that puppy real quick.

To get the mood right, I sprayed myself with a little Obsession perfume. By the time I pulled up my skin-tight denim jeans it was 5:50, so I grabbed the heap of clothes and threw them in the closet. After a quick dab of red lipstick, I played around with my braids to make sure I had no foreign objects sticking to any hair strands.

I said, "All right, Michelle, here we go. Do your thing." I smoothed out my pants, tugged at my shirt, smiled, and nodded. "With your fine self."

"Hey, gorgeous," Daryl said, moments after opening his door.

My plan to stay cool flew out the window when I saw that man. It didn't make any sense. One hundred percent panty-drop-on–the-first-night material standing over me. Like a giant Hershey's kiss waiting to be unwrapped.

Did I mention I love chocolate?

Again our eyes traveled every which-a-way, surveying each other's glorious assets. A beige nylon shirt hugged his thick chest. De-li-cious. I noticed he wore sandals, too. Hmmm. Nicely manicured toes-- no long pitchfork nails that could poke a hole in your thigh. Daryl definitely got an "A" for grooming. The chino pants seemed a bit too baggy, but it didn't taint his "fineness" at all.

I said, "No, you're the gorgeous one."

"Thanks." He smiled, then stepped back so I could enter. "You can go 'head and have a seat. Dinner's almost ready. By the way, thanks for coming over."

I blushed when he said that. I bet my cheeks stretched to the highest point a smile could go.

"Thanks for inviting me," I said. "I must say I've never had a man cook for me before."

He closed the door. "I'm happy to be the first."

I looked away, tugging on my braids. I don't know why I felt so nervous. I was struggling to maintain my composure and keep from unraveling into a giddy fool.

Once inside, I took a quick whiff. Mmmmm, whatever it was smelled pretty damn good—even better knowing it came from a man's kitchen. Culinary skills on blast. I couldn't wait to sample the goods.

Homeboy did his thing on the apartment, too. Boxes all gone and the place—spotless.

I peeked into the kitchen. Saw a wok filled with what looked like chicken stir-fry and a bowl of lettuce and tomatoes on the counter. "I see you doing your thing up in here. Smells good."

"Thank you," he said, walking back into the kitchen. "You want something to drink?"

When he asked that, my ears picked up an NBA announcer on the tube. I turned and saw game three of the NBA Finals. How in the world did I forget about the NBA Finals? Probably 'cause Daryl had occupied all corners of my mind since the moment I laid eyes on him.

I set my purse on the couch, sat down and became wrapped up in Lebron James shuttin' down my boy Tim Duncan. Wasn't lookin' too good for my team.

"Oh, man," I said, "I can't believe I forgot!"

"Me, too. I figured we can watch the game instead of the movies for now. Cool with that?"

"That's fine."

"Good. Now are you going to tell me what you want to drink?"

I chuckled. "I'm sorry. No, I'm fine. Thank you, Daryl."

When my future-husband Tony Parker made a shot, I damn near had a fit. "Wooo!" I screamed, pumping my fists. "That's what I'm talkin' 'bout!"

I pretty much lost all femininity. Took me a second, but once I realized where the hell I was, I jolted my silly ass back to reality.

Cupping a hand over my mouth, I turned to the kitchen. Daryl was leaning against the refrigerator, his face crunched up from laughing so damn hard.

I couldn't help but giggle, too. "I'm sorry. Got a little carried away. I love me some Tony Parker."

"No, don't apologize! I like to see competitive fire in a woman. Don't hold back." He pointed at the TV. "But don't be mad when my team whips dat ass. They gonna win tonight."

I looked at him, mouth all wide, playing the "I'm shocked" role. I admit, the Heat were beatin' up on my team, but the series wasn't over, yet.

"Whatever!" I cried. "They may win the game, but we're gonna win the series!"

We went back and forth for a moment. It got a little loud as we ranted loyalty for our teams. After the way we connected in the gym, my comfort level had reached a point where it seemed we could scream at each other and still be okay.

Damn, we clicked.

Damn, I was horny.

Damn, I'm pitiful.

"Are you ready to eat?" he asked.

I smiled. Hadn't heard a man say that to me since ... damn, never. "Yes."

"Cool. I'll fix you a plate."

I stood, walked to the kitchen counter, and checked out the beautiful sight of a man who knew the ins and outs of the kitchen. With his back to me, Daryl placed brown rice and stir-fry on two plates. Shoot, forget the Finals. I put the game on visual pause for a moment; I had to check out Daryl again for the umpteenth time.

"Smells pretty good," I said, just to let him know I was standing at the counter and not staring, which you and I know was a lie. "You really can throw down."

He turned, his lips curved into a smile. I placed my elbow on the counter and cradled my head in my hand.

He stroked his chin. "Well, my mama taught me a thing or two, ya know."

Again I tried to peek at the booty, but not with those loose pants. Damn.

"What would you like to drink with your food?" he asked, opening the fridge. "I got some Pepsi, Smirnoff Ice—"

"Is that Riesling?" I pointed to a wine bottle on the counter.

He chuckled. I noticed a wicked glint in his eye. "Where'd that come from? My bad. I forgot that was there."

"Uh-huh," I said, nodding. "Whatever. You know that's my favorite wine. You ain't slick."

He remembered. Not bad. At the gym, I had confessed that a good Riesling would have a sista tipsy in no time. Only mentioned it once, but apparently he packaged that message and stored it in the back of his mind. Daryl had bought my magic potion on the sneak tip.

Now all I needed was his magic wand.

"I'm not gon' lie," I said, chewing the last bit of brown rice, "that was really good. You might have me beat."

And I wasn't just trying to pump up his ego. Homeboy did his thing in the kitchen for real.

He wiped the side of his lips with a napkin. "Thank you, thank you. Glad you liked it. It's your turn to show me a little sumn' sumn' now."

Oh, I'll show you something, all right. "I can do that. Can't wait."

We were sitting on the floor, just chillin', watching the game with trays in our laps. Even had the coffee table pushed back, shoes off, legs stretched out—the whole nine. Nice and comfortable. It felt good to let my hair down in front of a man. I was having fun.

We were acting the *fool*, too. Cuss words catapulted from our mouths as we screamed at the TV screen trying to referee the game. Tony Parker was having a good night, but my team? Blah! Not so good. Of course, Daryl talked smack nonstop. Punk.

It was cute, though. But you know what? Having innocent fun is one thing, but I was ready to do some not-so-innocent thangs. A sista was ready to cross the line, break some rules. Somethin'!

I leaned my head and shoulders against the sofa cushion, which made my breasts poke up through my blouse. The Riesling talked smack to a sista, too, stirring an intense vibe, urging me to "get dirty." I was ready for Daryl to douse my fire.

Hmmmm. Riesling, Daryl, and me. Talk about a freaky ménage-à-trois.

I glanced at Daryl as he threw back his last sip of wine. Watched how his bicep flexed when he raised his arm. Shoot, even the way his Adam's apple bobbed up and down when he swallowed was sexy. I was officially in heat.

That's when another devious act loomed in my head. The Riesling gave me courage to perform my next sneak move.

I took another sip. "Brrrrr!" I said as I lowered the glass, shuddering as liquid lava spread inside. My exaggerated outburst and the apparent lack of control of my hand caused wine to spill all over my two babies.

I performed my "damn, I'm so clumsy" act to a T, eyes wide with fake humiliation, mouth all open, ya know. I put the glass down on the table and tugged at my blouse. I was about to rise when Daryl moved his tray, got on all fours, and reached for the paper towel that I had "forgotten" was by my calf.

"It's aw'ight," he said. "I gotcha."

I gotcha, too. He came within a breath's distance of my body. He set his hands on both sides of my legs, forming a bridge over me. For a hot second I thought about snaking my hand under his shirt and around his butt accidentally-on-purpose. I brushed that thought away quick, though. I figured within the next few minutes I'd be able to play with his goodies all I wanted.

An aftershave mist washed over me. Yummy. I inhaled a large dose of that sweet smell. Shoot, I couldn't take it anymore. I decided to break my rule and make the first move.

As he grabbed the paper towel, I lifted my arm and curved my hand around the side of his face. Didn't say a word—just touched him. He stopped as my nails stroked his cheek, drawing love lines that mapped toward his jaw.

Okay, maybe lust lines.

His bottom lip dropped, eyelids fluttering as he followed the path of my hand. For a second I thought he would pull away, but he didn't. Slowly, he shifted his head my way and our eyes met. His dark pupils had a coffee-colored tint—and they had me hooked. I didn't hear the TV or anything else.

Here we go.

A tiny space and a lot of opportunity divided us. I slid my hand around the back of his head as he leaned those luscious lips toward me; lips that my tongue had yearned to bathe. Heat rushed from my face to the crevice between my breasts, my heart beats pounding out a rhythm like a rock drummer on speed. I couldn't wait to do a horizontal "cha-cha" so our love taps could merge and produce a rhythm of our own. I closed my eyes and...

Contact!

Now, I've never been high before, but with wine in my veins and Daryl's tongue in my mouth, I bet what I felt was about the same. I swear, once our lips united, jolts racked my body. It almost felt like he had entered me somewhere *else*. Damn, he tasted good. It had been a while since I kissed a man with passion in my heart.

Our mouths slow-danced—the lip-lock mambo as I liked to call it. Ooooh, it was beautiful. My first kiss. With Daryl.

In the midst of a sloppy one, we both forgot about the tray on my lap. He banged it with his knee and *clack!* The noise damn near scared the shit out of me. We broke apart.

Dag-nabbit! Before my damsel-in-distress act, I could've at least moved that thing out of my freakin' way.

"Oops," he said, flustered. "Sorry about that. Let me get this thing out of here."

We chuckled. Both of us, a little embarrassed, I think. Not exactly the kind of thing you want to happen while lost in someone else's flavors. He picked up the tray and shot me a wink.

As Daryl walked toward the kitchen, I figured I shouldn't let the moment fade away. Forget that. I wanted to add more fuel to the flame we'd created. NBA Finals my ass.

I used the sofa for support and got to my feet. I must've stood too fast 'cause that woozy-wobbly sensation clogged up my head and vision. I rested my hand on the armrest.

"Wooo! I'm buzzin'! Told you Riesling does this to me."

Daryl burst out laughing. He was loading the dishwasher when he saw my near-collision with the floor. "Watch out there, now!" he said. "Don't fall."

"I think I already have," I wanted to say.

When I regained my senses, I picked up his tray and stepped toward the kitchen. I placed the tray on the counter next to the other one.

"Thank you," he said, smiling.

I smiled, but didn't say one word. My body wanted to talk now. Grabbing his hand, I pulled him toward me. Re-introduced his lips to mine, savoring every sample. Pressing my breasts into his torso, I wrapped my hands around his waist, then slid one up his back and another to his ass. Time to feel the magic stick.

Yes, you heard me right. I had *no* shame. It was about to happen when...

"Michelle, we need to stop. We're going too fast."

What?

When I didn't respond, he placed his hands on my shoulders and stepped back. "We have plenty of time for this. Let's stop."

Say what, say huh?

My ears finally made contact with my brain, and I just kinda stood there for a good five seconds, staring into his puppy dog eyes. Something wasn't right. What man tells a woman to stop? I didn't know what to freakin' say. Face twisted up to the highest level of stupified. I mean, what the hell just happened here?

I must've blinked my eyes a dozen times. Finally, I asked, "Daryl, what's wrong?"

He didn't respond. Just walked around the island until I could only see the upper half of his body. I was like, *What the hell? He's walking away from me?*

With his head down, he said, "I just think we need to cool out ... so we don't do something we regret."

I shook. *Regret? Regret what?*

I put one hand on my hip and the other on the kitchen counter. Glared at him with eyes reduced to slits. Girl, I couldn't figure out what transpired between our first kiss to "we need to stop."

I sucked in air to calm the rage. "Daryl," I said, tapping my fingers on the counter, "Is there something wrong? I thought we were having a good time. Do you want me to stay or not?"

He raised his head like a child. "Yes, I really, *really* want you to stay." He looked away for a second, then back at me. "That's why you should leave."

What the ... didn't I hear that in a movie somewhere?

Wow. *Wow.* I wanted to go smooth off 'cause he had jacked up my natural high *and* my Riesling high. Got my hormones all out of order. Damn. Took a lot of freakin' self-control to keep my tongue in check.

To diffuse the situation, I said, "Fine. Whatever. I'll go."

I whipped my ass around, grabbed my purse off the couch, and jetted toward the door. I made an about-face 'cause I wasn't fixin' to walk my ass outside without my shoes. Once I strapped on my sandals, Michelle got ghost. I heard him call my name but I'd gone deaf on him.

I flew down the stairs, titties double-dribbling up to my chin. Heard his door close, but I was already on the sidewalk hot-footin' back to my apartment. If I had let out all the fury screaming in my head through my mouth the whole damn block would've called the cops on me.

I can't believe this. What the hell just happened? Sorry ass. Man, I really like ... liked him, too. Ain't this a—

"Michelle, wait!"

Scared the shit out of me when he yelled. I didn't turn around, though, just kept truckin'. I was up the first two steps to my apartment when I replied, "Why? You told me to leave."

Daryl followed me. "Will you please stop? Damn, you fast."

He was closing in on me, creeping up on my ass. When I got to my door, I was a mess—huffing, puffing, forehead greasy from spots of sweat. I tried to play it cool when I faced him.

Before I could say another word, he said, "Look. I'm sorry, okay?"

Except for the movement of my chest jerking air in and out, all my other hyperactivity halted. I gazed into a pair of dark eyes that begged for forgiveness, feeling the strength in his hands when he caressed my shoulders.

He said, "I don't want to move too fast, Michelle. As much as I want to, I just..." He looked away, then rolled his eyes until his head faced the cement.

Daryl had me at "I'm sorry."

I slipped his hands off my shoulders and knotted our fingers together. After I inhaled, I said, "Daryl, you really caught me off guard. I was just going with the moment. We're two consenting adults, right?"

He nodded. "Yes. But..."

"But, what?"

Daryl crunched his eyebrows together. I could sense his discomfort. He said, "Let's just say I ... I don't want to ... it's just too early." He raised his hand to my face and stroked my cheek. Stared into me so deep I swear he seized my soul. "Can we wait a while, baby?"

Lawd, I melted when he said that. The way he said "baby" in a voice even deeper than Barry White's ... goodness. That one word swept away any remnant of anger I had. Pushed the corners of my frown upside down.

And why the hell was I angry, anyway? Hormones and alcohol, boy, I tell ya. Bad combo, sometimes—especially for me. When I came to my senses and saw the big picture, I was actually glad he stopped me. I probably came off like such a slut. Damn, Michelle.

I relaxed my shoulders and sighed. "All right, all right. I'm the one who needs to apologize for being so aggressive and all. I have to admit, I respect you for that. Not too many brothas are like you."

He chuckled. "In more ways than one, I can tell you that."

"Huh?"

"Nothin', nothin'. So, are we fine?"

I rolled my eyes, but smiled. "Yes, we're fine."

"Good. I'm gonna go, okay?"

Hormones took me hostage again. I wanted to whine, plead, yell—do something to convince him to come in so I could give him a tour of my bedroom.

But I kept all that to myself.

"All right," I said softly, my anger diffused.

He smiled. When he leaned toward me, I tasted his juices one more time. Gave me one of those long, slow smackity-smack kisses. Yum-yum. The kind of kiss that'll make a girl dizzy. I had to push him off.

"Look here," I said, "you need to get gone unless you want me to drag you inside and handcuff your butt to my bed."

He chuckled. "Okay, okay, I'm going. I know we live across from each other, but can you give a brotha your phone number anyway?"

That shocked me for some reason. Kind of weird that I felt a love connection with this man, but he didn't even have my direct line. Shoot, the way I saw it, if I called him it would be because Michelle needed a nightcap.

But only when he was ready.

After I gave him my number, he said, "I'll see you, okay? You wanna hit the gym after work tomorrow?"

I nodded. "Sure. Let's do that."

He smiled, gave me another peck, then disappeared down the stairs. I leaned against my door, reflecting and recovering. I didn't know what to think 'cause my mind was stuck between contentment and confusion. Shoot, how many men you know will turn down a hassle-free invitation to coochie? When he rejected me, it screwed me all up 'cause that just doesn't happen in "da real world," ya know?

But as I stared off into space, lost in my own world, I began to feel ... I don't know ... secure, I guess. Kinda felt like I'd found "the one." Daryl was obviously a man who cared enough to tap on the brakes so we could ease into something deeper than just an occasional booty-bump.

And he did say, "We'll have plenty of time for this." I liked the sound of that.

So I opened my door and whisked my horny ass in the apartment. After climbing into bed, I was about to reach for the toy in my nightstand to release the build-up of tension, but decided to call Charlotte first.

That was a mistake.

Chapter 9

"*He* said ya'll were moving too fast?" Charlotte asked. I could see her beady eyes doubling in size. "Well, that's different."

I sighed. "Yeah ... well ... I should respect that, I guess. We *were* going too fast. I've only known the man since yesterday, damn."

"True. But that's exactly what men want. Rip off your pants before they even know your name."

I laughed. "Not all men, apparently."

"Is he deeply religious or something?"

"I don't think so. I've heard a few curse words here and there."

"Ex-wife?"

"What? No. No kids, either. At least, that's what he said."

She paused. Probably tapping her finger on her lip. "Hmmm. Interesting."

I crossed my leg over my knee and turned the TV down. "Damn, girl. Stop analyzing! Oops, I forgot—you're *always* doing that!"

"Whatever. You know that's why your ass called me. Hmmm. I think he's hiding something. You said he bought Riesling, right? You lost your virginity on that stuff, didn't you?"

Damn, I forgot I'd told her that. "Yeah. Why?"

"You must've told him how tipsy it makes you, right?"

"Yeah. What's your point?"

"He had a plan, girl! Dine you, wine you, and get behind you!"

Chuckles rushed out of my mouth. "Charlotte, shut up! We didn't do it, remember?"

"Yeah, 'cause he had a conscience attack! That fool hidin' something, I'm telling you! As fine as you say he is, that just doesn't sound right to me."

"Why not?"

"'Cause, girl! Why else would he set the mood like that? He was planning on getting some boo-tay." She paused. I heard her breath brush against the receiver. Then she 360'd on me and said, "Well, I don't know. Maybe he does want to take his time. But remember those guys you dealt with in the past? All of them had serious issues, right? Daryl probably isn't any different."

I frowned. That was a low blow. "Damn, girl, that's messed up."

She paused. "Look, I didn't mean anything by that. His reaction just seems a little odd to me. I'm not used to guys responding like that. You know how suspicious I am."

I glanced at the muted TV screen and watched some woman's finger and mouth move so fast I could tell she was cursing out the man who faced her. "Yeah ... you are. That's why it took you five years to marry Greg. And he asked you two years into the relationship."

"Your butt needs to be more like that, too," she snapped. "What the hell were you doing all up in a man's apartment you didn't know, anyway? All by yourself, too! That fool could've been the black Ted Bundy. Damn, didn't I teach you anything?"

Wow. That didn't cross my mind at all. Kinda pissed at myself that it didn't.

I bit my fingernail, flashing to when Daryl asked me to bring his lamp up. How we were all alone in his apartment. How I was so wrapped up in him that I didn't use common sense. A fine ass man made me too damn trusting within seconds of meeting him.

"Chelle? You still there?"

I shook. "Yeah, yeah, I'm here." I coughed, then switched gears. "What's Greg doin'?"

"Shoot, what do you think? All night, every night I hear 'tap-tappity-tap' on that laptop. Can't wait 'till he finishes. He's up to 308 pages."

"Damn, that's a lot. I wish I could write a book. Be nice if he sells it, huh?"

"Yes! Especially before the baby comes."

"Right, huh? Damn, yo' ass is pregnant. Any baby names, yet?"

"Oh, yeah!" Her voice got all high and excited. "We were just looking through a book of names, too. If it's a girl, we were thinking Tia; a boy, maybe something like Ross. I like Jewel, too. He likes Quen for a boy. Shoot, we might just use our names. Then again..."

I let her ramble on. Only name on my mind was Daryl.

"What do you think, Chelle?"

"Huh? Oh, I don't know. Long as it doesn't end with a 'qua', you'll be okay."

She laughed. "I know that's right. Ghetto name like Lashanifiqua. Or some car name like Porsche or Mercedes."

"Yeah, none of that," I said, giggling. "Stay away from the liquor names, too. I don't want my godbaby named something crazy like Hennessey or Alizé."

"Or Riesling!" Charlotte chimed in.

We collapsed in giggles.

Charlotte caught her breath. "Seriously though, you sure you all right? You're not upset that I'm doubting your man, are you?"

"No, no." I sighed. "Although, you do realize you're dissing him before even meeting him."

She sighed. "I know. I wasn't trying to pee on your leg. I'm just saying be careful. Like I said, he could be Ted Bundy in black. Or Jeffrey Dahmer. Ew! Or—"

"Will you shut up?" I rolled my eyes. "Say hi to Greg for me. I'll see you at work tomorrow."

She smacked her tongue. "Forget work. I'm not going."

I laughed. "See you at work tomorrow. Love ya."

"Love you, too. Goodnight."

"Goodnight."

I hung up the cordless and flung it on the bed, sighing and staring at the TV, but my mind was somewhere else, conjuring up dumb shit. Like wondering if Daryl had chopped up body parts packed in his freezer. Damn.

Damn, damn, *damn!*

Why did I call that ho?

Chapter 10

It's funny how friends can make you have second thoughts. Charlotte jacked me up big time—to the point where doubt rung in my head.

My supervisor had been tied up in meetings all day, which gave me plenty of uninterrupted time to finish an important PowerPoint presentation, but my date with Daryl the night before kept cutting into a sista's focus. I really wasn't getting much done.

As I sat at my desk, staring at the monitor, I broke away from my Daryl fantasy and let reality blanket over me. Damn Charlotte and her cautionary tales—a sista couldn't even romanticize around her.

I had found my black knight, a man with a deep, velvety voice who swept me away from a horde of male vermin. A man who wined and dined me with a simple plate of stir-fry and Riesling. A man who made me long for the moment when he would part my seas and deep-stroke within my channel ... all damn night.

But now, instead of seeing the potential in this fine-ass man, I second-guessed every damn thing—all because I listened to Charlotte.

I hate that ho.

Why did I call her ass, anyway? I should have known better. Charlotte has always been one of those skeptical types. Just asking questions all the time. Why this? Why that? While I'm more of an it-is-what-it-is type. Ain't no need to analyze all the damn time.

But there I was, analyzing like a mofo. Shoot, I had made up stuff to poke, prod and probe, like some damn forensic scientist.

Damn! I *hate* that ho!

She had sabotaged sweet images of Daryl and me standing in his living room, our schoolyard stares scanning each other, me touching him for the first time. Fortunately, I had brushed away all the sexual predator thoughts, but now I was thinking what the hell was he hiding? I mean, really, why did he back off like that? Then he asked me to leave! What kinda shit is that? Was something wrong with me? With him?

Questions sprouted like weeds, so you know what that meant. Yup. Now that I had doubts and all these questions, I needed answers, so I got nosy. Donning my private eye hat, I Googled a brotha, but didn't find anything that set off alarm bells. Then I went to his job's website. Still came up short, though. That's when a wild idea bopped me upside my head:

I should go to that fool's job to see if he even works there.

I know. Idiotic stuff.

I left work at four and sped toward the 15-South. My gaze stuck to the road but Daryl's beautiful face-body-voice and Charlotte's speech played tug-of-war in my mind.

Got caught on the 52-West parking lot for thirty minutes. California traffic always found a way to piss me off, especially with my pantyhose cuttin' into a sista's thighs. While I waited, I took off my pumps and let 98.1 FM Jazz ease my anxiety.

Finally cars spread out and the traffic jam opened up. I took 5-North, then the Sorrento Valley exit.

Time to get CSI up in here.

What the hell am I doing here again?

I'd parked in a football field-sized lot facing the front entrance, camped out somewhere in the middle. I was close enough to verify his face once he walked out, but I pulled out my mini binoculars from the glove compartment just in case.

Yes, *bi-no-cu-lars.*

That's some shit, huh? Known him for two days and already stalking him. What the hell was I doing in *my* car with a quarter tank of gas at *his* job at 4:57 with *my* seat pushed back and binoculars in *my* hands? I'd lost my damn mind.

Every time the glass doors opened, my heart jumped. But no Daryl.

"This is ridiculous," I said, sighing. "I need to stop."

I glanced at the rearview mirror. Damn, such a hot mess. Braids Grace Jones wild from driving with the window down. Moisture seeped under my arms, making my Secret not so secret.

A heavy dose of common sense penetrated my thick skull. "Hel-lo?" I said to my reflection. "What are you doing here?"

I let a few four-letter words have their way as I pulled my seat back up. Jamming the key in the ignition, I turned to the front entrance one last time.

My jaw dropped. *I'll be damned.*

I rushed the binoculars to my eyes and witnessed the undeniable. I thought my head would explode from the swift flow of blood. My eyelids lowered to half-mast. Couldn't believe what lay before me, but at the same time, I could.

I sighed. "Figures."

I collapsed against the seat, deflated. Leaning my chair back again, I closed my eyes. Yeah, he worked there all right, but I damn sure didn't expect *that!*

What, you ask?

A wife and two kids, that's what.

This penny brown-skinned woman in a dark-blue skirt suit walked next to Daryl looking kids-at-a-playground happy. The stubby teenage boy in the NIKE hat beside them didn't really resemble Daryl much. Neither did the skinny young sista in the red dress. I could tell those two scooped up most of Mama's genes. Or maybe they were his step-kids?

Didn't matter—family is family, and they definitely looked like one big ass happy family.

Ugh, why did he have to look so damn fine, too? He wore black slacks and a white button down shirt with a dark tie. Looked like one of those models you see gracing department store brochures.

But married. *Mar-ried*, you hear me?

Daryl placed his hand on the boy's neck. The kid made some gesture with his fingers. Whatever that meant, it made Daryl grab his cap and pull it down over his face. After that, Daryl pinched his daughter's cheek. She slapped his hand away, smiled, then wrapped her thin arms around him.

My stomach swirled.

I watched how he and his wife laughed and carried on, engaged in a verbal intercourse that seemed much like the kind of connection I thought *we* had. Made me feel violated—like *she* robbed *me* of something. But you can't steal something that already belongs to you. I was the other woman here—not her.

Daryl held his wife's hand. When she stepped down the stairs, her curls danced in front of her face. A pretty woman, I admit; she seemed classy and intelligent, but older. Had Daryl by at least ten years. Kids were cute, too.

The woman turned to Daryl. When Daryl leaned toward her, I pulled the binoculars from my face, turned away, then slumped into my chair.

I know, I know. I was tripping. Don't know why, either. It ain't like he was *really* mine, right? But when you're feelin' someone, how else do you react?

I don't know how long I stared at my car's interior, but when I looked out the window, Daryl and his family had vanished.

Crazy thoughts raged in my brain once again: *What do I do now? Confront him? Ignore him? Damn! Why he gotta be married?*

I didn't want to get caught in the mix, ya know? Couldn't see my butt scrambling for my robe at two in the morning with sista-girl at my door cursing Daryl and me to high hell with both her kids at her side crying their eyes out. I may be a lot of things, but a homewrecker, I'm not. Forget that.

Well, it was fun while it lasted. Homegirl can keep his scandalous ass 'cause I'm through with him.

Chapter 11

I *thought* I was through with him.

Kind of hard to be out-of-sight, out-of-mind when our apartments are damn near holding hands, but I avoided him the best I could. Didn't answer his phone calls, respond to knocks on the door, acknowledge the flower he left on my welcome mat—nothin'. By Tuesday night, I'd deleted four messages from my answering machine. With each message, I noted the hurt in his voice.

Hmmph! That's what his ass gets!

But hold on now. Can't forget the flip side.

I could run, hide, even send smoke signals that said "leave me the fuck alone," but I still couldn't evict his sexy butt from my mind. Daryl had latched on to my inner core, and I felt like I'd need a damn exorcism to yank him out of my system. I didn't want to let the possibility of what we could become go. Hell, we hadn't even started anything yet, really.

I could hear the hurt in his voice—an ache I had apparently caused. But as much as I wanted, I refused to relent. He had a *wife!* And *kids!* Still, the resonance of his apologies seduced my ears. Made my whole body squirm for relief.

Wasn't long before I made excuses *for* Daryl. I mean, hell, his family didn't live with him, so obviously he and his wife were separated. Maybe even divorced, but kept it cordial for the kids' sake. But if that was the case, why did he tell me he didn't have kids? I damn near made myself half-crazy with the "what ifs." My hyper analysis went off—I felt like that damn Charlotte, asking why, what, who, when and friggin' where.

But hearing his voice slowly chipped away at my brick wall. Made me feel bad for avoiding him. Shoot, he had no idea *why* he was apologizing, actually. I could have at least given him that.

Of course, that justified my seeing him again.

So, when I got to my apartment that Wednesday afternoon, I couldn't hold back my wide smile when I saw the yellow sticky on my door that said, "Michelle, please call me when you get in. I have a surprise for you."

I went straight to the phone. After I kicked off my heels, I plopped on the couch, took in a long breath and tried to get into bitch mode. Had to get my guard back up, ya know.

The phone rang three times. When he said "hello," I swallowed.

"It's me."

"Michelle? Hey! Hold on for a sec."

I heard somebody in the background singin' "don't mess with my man." Hmmph. That's exactly how I felt but didn't have the right.

"Are you in the car?" I asked.

The radio faded. "Yeah. Had my phone forwarded this morning in case you called."

Whoa. He had forwarded his phone calls ... just for me. Bitch mode took a hit.

I curled my lips, trying to unravel a smile. "So, are you on your way home?"

"Yes. Where you been the past few days? Seems like you're avoiding me."

I thought I'd prepared myself for that question. In my mind I had the verbal bullets ready, but my mouth jammed. I couldn't just come out with "I was on a stakeout at your job when I saw you, your wife and two kids."

I nibbled my finger. "Um ... well ... wait till you get home. I'll talk to you then." I punched the couch pillow.

Silence for a few seconds. Then he asked, "Is everything all right?"

I felt my hard stance falling. Yeah, right. What hard stance?

"Yes," I said, "I'll see you when you get here."

"Okay. I'll trust you on that. I take it you got my little sticky?"

Had it in my hand. I loved the way his cursive scribble looped the letters in my name. I raised my smile higher. "Yes."

"Good. Okay, well, I'm about fifteen minutes away, so I'll see you in a few, all right? Can you be at my place by 6:30?"

I looked at my watch. It was nearly 5:45. "Yes, I'll be there."

"Aw'ight, then. I'll check you later. Don't forget, now."

"I won't."

And that was the end of that.

Damn. I was supposed to be pissed, but that didn't work. How the hell could I even think about putting up a pissed-off façade with that man's voice floating through me?

I threw my back against the sofa and closed my eyes. "All right. We'll see what this surprise is first, and *then* I'll tell him what I know!"

Had that all wrong, too.

I cracked my knuckles. Had those bad boys sounding like popcorn.

Daryl opened the door. His face became Las Vegas-at-night bright when he set his eyes on me. "Well, well, well. How are you?"

I tried to hold my stone-faced expression, but couldn't. He wore a sleeveless dashiki-looking outfit that had an urban edge to it. Saying he looked good is the understatement of the millennium.

He noticed my eyes checking him from head to sandals. "You like this, huh? Got it at an African store downtown. Thought I'd try it on."

I smiled and somehow managed a dry, "Looks nice."

As I walked in, I tried to muster the courage to tell him that I knew about his family, but I didn't have to. Why?

His two kids were sitting on the couch.

If that was the surprise, then that's a surprise for yo' ass.

I held back the cuss words circling in my head, but the questions kept mounting: *Okay, he told me he didn't have kids, but brought me over to meet kids he said he didn't have? What kinda sense does that make?* The dots didn't connect.

They waved. I shuddered. "Uh ... hi."

Daryl took my hand. "Kids, this is my friend Michelle."

Friend? My eyelids flapped. Somehow I faked a smile, but Daryl needed to get to the point quick. Hot blood started to singe my veins.

"That's Donald and his sister, Shanda. I just found out Donald passed all his exams and will be graduating with his classmates from Roosevelt High. Ceremony's next Saturday."

Graduate? I dug deep into the memory bank. Felt heat rush across my cheeks.

Then I remembered.

Daryl was Donald's Big Brother from the Big Brothers/Big Sisters program. He had told me all about Donald in the gym.

You woulda thought somebody yanked my face apart the way my mouth dropped open and eyes widened. "Oh! Boy, get over here and give me a hug!"

Don't ask me why I did that. I guess I was relieved that Daryl didn't have a pre-packaged family on the side.

Donald read me up and down, turning his head a little. I walked to him with my wings spread. He stood.

I wrapped him up. "Congratulations, baby!"

His forehead bumped my nose. I realized why I thought he was a pre-teen. He was barely 5'6" tops.

Damn, what a relief! I must have squeezed him too tight 'cause he grunted. But then he got a little too comfortable, snaking his arms around my back close to the danger zone.

"Boy, don't try to be slick, now," Daryl said. "Get them hands up."

Donald stepped back, hands in the air, trying to play it cool. "What?"

Daryl wagged his finger. Let Donald know the deal with his eyes. "You know what."

"Yeah, boy," Shanda said, "you think just 'cause you 'bout to graduate you grown now. Hope you don't try to put your stinky hands on a bunch of females' butts after the ceremony."

We laughed. It felt good. Hadn't gotten my chuckle on in a while. The positive vibes in the room obliterated all doubt, and my respect for Daryl soared. So used to seeing men walk *away* from kids, yet here was Daryl, standing in and not afraid to play Papa to kids that weren't even his by blood.

Donald play-punched his sister. She pushed his hand away, stood, then doubled-up, fixin' to get Laila Ali on that ass.

When Donald bumped against the computer desk, Daryl said, "Hey! If you two mess up my living room I'll bust both of you!"

I stood in the background, watching the youngsters act their age. They were cute. I hadn't been around young adults in a minute.

But, boy, did I feel like one colossal *dumbass!* I had given up valuable time with Daryl because of a jacked up assumption. My paranoia had me acting a fool—creeping on his job, hiding out, imitating Inspector Gadget on crack.

Yeah, I ain't listening to Charlotte's ass again.

Shanda grabbed her purse off the table. "Okay, Daryl, we're getting out of here. The movie starts at 7:30."

Daryl grabbed his wallet off the kitchen counter and pulled out two twenty-dollar bills.

"Here," Daryl said, handing Donald the money, "buy some new pants or sumn'."

Donald frowned. "With forty bucks? What, you want me to buy one pant leg?"

I laughed. Daryl said, "I can take my money back, now."

"No, no, that's cool," Donald said, waving him off. "Thanks, Daryl." They hugged the way men do when trying to be macho.

Shanda held out her hand. "Where mine at?"

Daryl smiled. "When you graduate from UCSD, I'll hook you up."

"That's cold," she said.

Daryl grabbed her hand, unballed his fist, and dropped two twenties into her palm, too. Her big smile exposed smooth, white teeth.

Shanda wrapped her pencil arms around his back, the same innocent move that riled me up before. "Thank you."

While Daryl and Shanda hugged, I ignored Donald x-raying me. I knew that boy wanted to bend me over and tap my booty like a little drummer boy. Couldn't blame him though. His teenage hormones were probably just as out of whack as mine.

Daryl opened the door. "All right, guys, get on outta here."

Shanda turned to me. "It was nice to meet you, Michelle."

"You too, Shanda. Good luck with school."

"Yes," Donald said, "very nice." He grabbed my hand. When he leaned down to kiss it, Daryl slid his hands under his mouth. Donald's lips collided with Daryl's knuckles.

Donald tried to wipe away the stink of male skin from his lips. We all busted up laughing. "Man, why you do that?"

"You know why," Daryl said, edging him out the door. "Trying to push up on her. That's my job. Get on outta here."

I waved goodbye while guilt corroded my insides. Daryl closed the door and faced me. "Well, that was my surprise." He frowned a little, staring. "You all right?"

I lowered my head. Didn't want him seeing the shame that distorted my face.

"I ... I'm fine," I replied. While raising my head back up, beads of moisture formed in the corner of each eye. "I'm proud of what you've done. What a difference you must've made in his life. If it wasn't for you, he probably wouldn't be graduating, huh?"

Daryl shrugged. "Possibly. He's a good kid. All he needed was some adult male guidance to keep him out of trouble—especially with his mom being a single parent and all."

I was still kinda nosy, so I asked, "What's their mom like?"

"Cool woman. Had some issues with drugs in the past, but things have definitely turned around for her, too. They came by my job on Monday to tell me she's been promoted to Assistant Sales Manager at her appliance company."

I stood quiet, reflecting on my silly ways. Had it all wrong *again*. No wifey, no baby mama. "So, you've been his Big Brother for a year?"

"Just about. When I first started working with Donald, he was struggling through summer school so he could start his senior year instead of having to repeat the 11th grade. I did homework with him, helped him study, gave him money if he passed a test—the whole nine. He passed all his classes, barely." He wiped away a tear stream from my face with his thumb. "Are you sure you're all right?"

I inhaled. "I'm fine. Just fine."

The corners of my lips couldn't rise any higher. Daryl had peeled away more layers surrounding him, revealing an unselfish man concerned about impacting our youth in a positive way. I only saw a glimpse of his influence on Donald, but within minutes of meeting Donald and his sister, it's obvious we need more Daryls in the world, especially for young brothas Donald's age. Way too many sperm donors leaving young boys and girls who become loose cannons, fending for themselves and expecting Baby Mama to pick up all the slack by her damn self. Sorry ass men.

But not Daryl. The more I realized how wrong I was about him, the stupider I felt for placing Daryl in the same category as the idiots I'd dated in the past.

He kissed my cheek, then grabbed a tissue off the counter and handed it to me. "So, Ms. Larsen, how come I haven't heard from you? We were supposed to work out, remember? Came by your apartment a few times, but no answer. I figured you were ignoring a brotha. Did I do something?"

"Huh? Oh ... let's just say I was being stupid. I jumped to some silly conclusions, but promise to never do it again. Can we leave it at that?"

He walked toward the kitchen sink. "Conclusions, huh? Ooookay. You sure everything's cool?"

"Yes, we're cool. I was trippin' about nothing, but that's done. I promise."

He opened the refrigerator door. "Aw'ight then. I'll leave it at that, but I need to let you in on a little sumn' important."

"What's that?"

"What's going to happen tonight."

"And what's going to happen tonight?"

"The Heat are going to get in dat ass. You didn't forget, did you?"

I smiled. Aww, the NBA Finals. With all my obsessing over Daryl and a wife I'd made up, I'd completely forgotten. I turned, flicked on the TV and flipped through the channels until I heard an NBA announcer. I also made a secret promise to not do any more dumb shit that could jeopardize what Daryl and I were building.

We gazed at each other, smiling. I took off my shoes and sat on the couch. Daryl sat down beside me and handed me a beer.

I took a sip. "Oh, you mind if I get sum a dat?"

"Some of what?"

"Sum a dat stuff you smokin' 'cause you know good and well your team ain't gonna do a damn thing tonight."

His eyes lit up. "Oh, so you got jokes? Aw'ight, whoever wins gets to ... um ... gets to..."

"Gets to cook dinner for a week."

He nodded. "Aw'ight, then."

We shook hands. I psyched myself up, gettin' ready to talk smack all night.

Daryl and Michelle take two. Things went back to normal and back on track ... kinda.

Chapter 12

Six beautiful weeks.

That's how long I'd been dating Daryl.

Five torturous months.

That's how long I'd gone without a little "stroke" action.

I guess the best word to describe my whatchamacallit with Daryl would be "confused." Scratching my damn head, trying to crack his code, but getting nowhere. I'd been doing a lot of that the past six weeks—and it was all Daryl's fault. I thought the guessing game stopped, but Daryl made me think of him as like a walking Jeopardy game show or some shit.

Now don't get me wrong—Daryl had done an A-plus job of wooing me and all. The men in my dreams didn't come close to what Daryl was bringing to the table in real life. I'd been on Cloud Nine times ten since we met and still hadn't come down. He kept his end of the bet, too—definitely no sore loser. After reminding him of our little arrangement—courtesy of the world champion San Antonio Spurs—I enjoyed a week's worth of homemade buffalo shrimp, macaroni and cheese, baked chicken, buttermilk biscuits, collard greens, corn bread—you name it. The man threw it down in the kitchen!

We did all the sweet things new couples do—held hands, sloppy kisses, three-hour phone conversations. So nice to spend time with a man on the same page, ya know? I enjoyed every moment we spent together, but for some reason, no stroke action.

We'd become workout buddies, so I saw him almost every day. Even introduced him to Charlotte and Greg and did the Netflix thing at their house once or twice. Of course, they loved Daryl. The first time Charlotte laid eyes on that Ebony Man face, all those concerns she had about him in the past ceased.

She was like, "You'd better handcuff his fine ass to your hip!"

But as close as we got ... still ... no stroke action. And I had *no* idea why. *None.*

A healthy man refusing to do the damn thang? With a fine-ass body like mine?

Yes. Believe it. Didn't make no damn sense.

What a tease, you hear me? Had my hormones slam-dancing all over the place, beggin' a sista for something hard to heal the "pain," but I refused anything that buzzed, vibrated, beeped, clicked—whatever! Hell, I didn't even use my own, up-to-the-job fingers when the mood hit. I kid you not. Nope. Not me.

All right, all right, you *know* I'm lyin'. Sometimes I resorted to a little, uh, "mechanical help." Batteries included. But I didn't want that! That was Daryl's job—if he would just come to work! Damn, why make a sista wait?

I told myself so many times I should be happy to have a man that didn't make sex a trivial thing. I'd say, "Michelle, wait until he's ready" or "I should respect his decision to wait" or "I want it to be special, just like he apparently does." Those words looped over and over in my head. But they were just words. Deep down I *felt* like a freakin' man because no matter what, I was still schemin' to get in his pants, ya know?

And yet, I didn't come out with a huge fuss because I figured just being a woman would eventually break him down. Part of me looked it as a challenge, especially since I knew he wouldn't last too long before our underwear dropped. Men are so weak for a nice booty and a smile.

I obviously got that wrong, though.

Daryl had a level of self-control I'd never seen in a man before. No matter how sneaky I was, nothing worked! Didn't matter what I wore, how nice I smelled, the sweet things I said—nothing I tried penetrated his wall of celibacy.

Nothing.

Nada.

Zero.

Zilch.

Damn!

What the hell was going on? I searched for answers as far as my warped brain would allow, each conclusion wilder than the next: he's found religion; he's gay; he has a disease; he's a hermaphrodite; his willy is no bigger than his nose and he's embarrassed to show it; he lost his penis in some heifer's coochie.

I even thought maybe his thing was deformed. Maimed in some crazy accident and didn't work anymore. Like maybe he stood too close to a weed wacker one day, it latched on to his pants, tore off his underwear then tangled his willy and ... well ... you can figure it out. Ouch.

Yes, my XXX-rated mind went nuts. Sometimes I felt like a First-Class ho, though—just couldn't shake the urge to tear his clothes off and act like a pair of lions in the jungle. Was I wrong to think like that?

Hell no. I'm a hot-blooded woman with *needs,* damnit!

Many times I had to resist the impulse to get bold and speak my mind. Just break it down for him like, "Daryl, cut this goody two-shoes crap out and fuck me! Damn!" Well, that thought remained just that—a thought.

Oh, well. Whatever the case, "baby girl" became a dark wet alley, bouncing echoes off her walls, trying to remind Daryl of her existence: *Yooooo hoooo! Peeeenisssss! Can you hear meeeee!*

No one could hear. Well, that no one being Daryl.

I did my best not to pressure him and just went with the flow, but after a month of dating, with each date still ending with a hug, kiss, and wave, a sista's patience was wearing thin, so enough was enough. Time to put an end to the G-rated playground ring-around-the-rosy shit. Fuck it. I recalibrated my new Daryl radar, primed to detect and dissect any oddity.

Time to get to the bottom of this whole penile restriction crap.

One Thursday afternoon, I scooted to the complex gym to meet Daryl and get my fitness on. I wore black leg warmers and a white tank top, exposing enough lady lumps to cause a few fender benders. As I neared the entrance, I noticed Daryl through a small gym window, standing behind some guy. A sista froze in her tracks. "What the..."

I squinted. Okay, he wasn't *behind* him, behind him—if you know what I mean. I saw a chair between them. Still, I paused my iPOD and peeked in. From their position, they couldn't see me.

The guy sitting in the chair, a medium-brown skinned brotha who looked short enough to tap his forehead against my chin, pushed two dumbbells upward. Daryl spotted him.

I was like, "Who is he?"

When brothaman finished the set, can you believe that fool looked up at Daryl and said, "Thanks, man. Hopefully I'll get cut like you one day." Then he shot Daryl a goofy smile.

Daryl smiled back at him and said, "Yeah, maybe one day." Then he laughed.

I frowned.

Now, I'm no genius, but a sista knows the anatomy of a flirt. Smiling, carryin' on, laughin' and what not. Hmmph. Any other day, I probably wouldn't raise an eyebrow. But six weeks, mind you, and Daryl had not attempted one taste of my coochie delight. Shoot, not even a whiff.

That's when it *really* hit me. Like someone had whipped my behind with a wet towel.

Maybe Daryl didn't even *like* coochie. You'd be hard-pressed to find a single man who wouldn't perform cartwheels for a daily dose of poontang ... unless ... well, you guessed it.

Aw hell. With that thought handcuffed to my brain, my radar became "gaydar." Could Daryl be ... downlow-ish? Wanting a different hole for the pole?

Nooooooooo. Not him.

Right?

But, six weeks with no push on the puss?

Fuck. Maybe.

I had to investigate. Pushing the door open, I walked in, cool as ice water. Daryl was putting the dumbbells up when I made my appearance.

"Hey, Daryl," I said.

I expected a deer-in-the-headlights look, but he turned toward me and said, "Hey, baby. Damn, lookin' all good as usual."

He grabbed my hand, reeled me in and jammed my Daryl gaydar with a smile and peck. Damn, girl. Cherry lips pressed against mine. Made me feel like a woman—*his* woman. He missed me. I could tell.

For a hot second, Daryl was no longer suspect. But then the five-footer stood up. He said, "Oh. I see you got your lady here."

I swore I smelled a hint of jealousy. I was like, *Yeah, Pip Squeak. And?*

Daryl said, "Yeah, Mike. This is my girl, Michelle. Michelle, Mike. Mike just moved here from San Francisco."

San Francisco? Aw hell. "Is that right?" I asked, with a raised eyebrow. "Welcome."

We shook hands. He said, "Thanks, sista."

I smiled, fake as hell, but shoot, he didn't know that. I had him by at least two inches. I looked down, my gaze locked on Mr. Mike, checking him out. Thin mustache, big eyes, stocky build. Cute, I guess. But on the down-low? Hmmmmmm. I wondered if he was Daryl's type. Damn, what *was* Daryl's type?

I didn't detect an overflow of sugar in Mike's tank, but from what I'd heard, guys on the down-low didn't "switch." They can be all masculine and stuff, so how can a woman weed them out if they blend right in?

Mike chuckled. "If you don't mind, I'd like my hand back."

Shit. "Oh, I'm sorry," I said, trying to laugh it off. I released his hand.

I caught Daryl's face all pushed in, eyes flaring. Oh, boy. I probably looked like *I* was flirting.

"Well, it's nice to meet you, Michelle."

I said, "Um, you, too."

Mike wiped his wet face with a towel and checked his watch. "All right, man. Gotta roll. I'll let ya'll do your thing."

"All right, man," Daryl said. "We'll hook up later."

Eyebrows shot up my forehead. *Hook up?*

Mike gave Daryl a pound. I watched. Like a hawk. Checked them out, how he looked at Daryl and Daryl at him. The smile. Or was it a smile? Some flicker of the eye, maybe? That guy on Oprah said the eyes could make a connection without speaking, like some silent freak-nasty agreement between men who want men.

Mike waved, then walked out. Just me and Daryl now.

Daryl turned to me. "All right, Michelle. What was that about?"

I played dumb. "What?"

"You know what. Staring at that dude, holding his hand. You were actin' funny, like you was 'bout to zap him with eye laser beams or sumn'."

I shook my head. Quick on my feet, I said, "Boy, if I was staring, it was because I'm not used to looking down at a man."

He laughed. "Oh, really? I thought you was—"

"So, how do you know Mike?"

He tilted his head, forehead wrinkled. Probably because I'd cut him off. Shoot, at the moment, I didn't care if that was rude. I had to interrogate!

"Damn, I told you he just moved in. We just started talkin' and hit it off." Daryl gave me the side eye. "Why?"

I walked toward an exercise bike and plopped my butt on the seat. "I was just wondering. You guys looked kinda tight."

Daryl stepped on the bike beside mine. "Yeah, he's cool. Turns out he works near me. And he's in the Computer Networking field, too. Cisco engineer. His wife and daughter are up north visiting her folks right now."

My head wobbled. "Wife and daughter? He's married?"

"Yes, when someone has a wife that usually indicates marriage. That allowed?"

I laughed. I didn't expect a family behind the scenes. Guess I'd jumped to the wrong conclusion. *Again.*

"Oh," I said. "Yes, that's allowed. Good for him."

Daryl pressed the timer for fifteen minutes. I did the same. Pre-workout warm-up ritual for us.

As I started pedaling, previews of the new Halle Berry movie yanked my eyes up for a hot second, co-starring a fine-ass brotha whose name I always forgot.

Daryl said, "There goes your boy. What's-his-name."

I shrugged. "He ain't all that."

"Yeah, whatever," Daryl said. "I know you all in loooove with him. I can see why women want him, though."

Gaydar came roaring back to life. I said, "You can, can you?"

"Yeah. He's a good lookin' guy."

Ding ding ding! Bells went off like an alarm at a firestation! But then he said, "I look better than him, though. Right, babe?"

I let out a breath. "Of course, babe."

He leaned toward me. Between our knees highsteppin' and feet burnin' the pedals, we kissed. Though Daryl was withholding the goods, he was always generous with the sweet, little gestures.

After a few more back-and-forths in my head, I finally brushed that nonsense away. No, he couldn't be on the down-low. But if not on the down-low, then what the hell?

Daryl said, "Hey, you wanna see that movie tomorrow night?"

"Hmmmm, sounds like a plan. I think Fashion Valley mall is showing it."

"Cool. Let's dress up and go out to dinner before the movie."

I smiled. "That sounds like a plan, too."

After Daryl and I got all Lance Armstrong on the bikes, we worked the dumbbells for another thirty minutes or so. Then we headed to his apartment, ordered a Papa John's pizza and popped in a DVD. When we finished the DVD, Daryl capped off the night with a kiss, wave and hug. *Again.* Same old shit.

What was this negro's issue? I made up my mind to find out after the movie. No more damn guessing games.

Chapter 13

I'd put in more than enough time and effort for my sure-to-be hot date with Daryl. As you know, he'd been pretty much hands off thus far—more PG-13 than R-rated and nowhere near XXX—but I had a feeling this particular night would change all that. After all, it was Freaky Friday!

So when he suggested we dress up for dinner, I went all out. I rummaged through my closet, pulled my little black dress out of retirement and matched it with a pair of silver stilettos. Lotioned up, scented up, lookin' and smellin' like a master skilled in instant hard-ons with a simple wink and a smile. No *way* Daryl would even think about sending me home alone tonight!

We made plans to eat at the Cheesecake Factory, then catch the 9pm showing of the movie afterward. We lived within walking distance of Fashion Valley, so we decided to hoof it. The soft breeze complimented the night sky. So beautiful out. Perfect for a lover's stroll, despite my stilettos.

And, damn, we looked good, like dark-skinned versions of Will Smith and Jada Pinkett. Nobody in San Diego tipped the fine-o-meter as high as Michelle and Daryl! No, not braggin', just statin' the facts.

Daryl wore a brown sports coat over a beige shirt with nice jeans—an outfit I helped pick out at the Men's Wearhouse. Talk about *tas-tee!* Lawd! Looked like homeboy was about to take the runway with Tyson Beckford.

I had it going on too, now. My black mini hugged my brick house frame in all the right places. Nice silver necklace with matching earrings straight from Tiffany's. Toes did, nails did, hair did. We looked so good we had everybody's eyes poppin'!

But it didn't take long before my Daryl radar straight acted the fool. What started out as a perfect date night took a turn south. Literally.

With Daryl's usual pimp limp next to my Tyra Banks stride, we chatted about this and that, primed for a long night of fun, laughter and hopefully "chocolate-flavored dessert." I was fumbling through my purse trying to find a mirror when I noticed something out of the corner of my eye. I'd seen it before, but never connected the dots. Until then.

Daryl was scratching between his legs.

My radar went "blip, blip, blip!"

Okay, Daryl's a guy. All men do it, I'm sure. Some men don't give a damn, scratching and cuffing their package in public like the shit 'bout to up and walk away or somethin'. To some degree, I understand. With all that "meat" crammed into tight, sweaty quarters, I'm sure underwear fabric gets a little itchy sometimes. Crotch like a summer day in Virginia and shit. Damn, what else can a brotha do? Cure that itch with a nice rubdown.

But as I ran through my mental rolodex, I realized Daryl was always scratching his sack. While watching a game, cooking, working out, walking.

Once again, Daryl's fingernails had their way for a few seconds, then went 'bout their business. Cool and calm, as natural as breathing. Didn't even break a sweat. Itch in, itch out—just like that.

My radar didn't like it, though.

After spot-checking my face and hair, I put away the mirror and zipped up my purse. Part of me listened to Daryl talking about Donald; the other part got all Agatha Christie on him.

Why was he *really* scratching himself? Was the source of the itch something other than tight underwear? Detection of an infection, maybe?

My stomach dropped. That was it. Had to be.

The more I paged my thoughts, the more it all made sense. He had something, and didn't know how to tell me. How do you reveal an incurable disease to a potential partner? An STD, at that?

As I pondered this new theory, I wondered if I could rock with someone who carried an STD. That thought floated around a bit, but as Daryl and I walked hand-in-hand, deep in an ambiance we created, I realized I already knew the answer.

We arrived at the Cheesecake Factory a few minutes later. A hostess showed us to a cozy little booth where we jammed our stomachs with Rigatoni and Fettuccini, drank a little chardonnay, had a good ol' time as usual. I swear, despite the chitter-chatter of a thousand patrons, the timbre of Daryl's deep-throat voice and bleach-white smile sucked away the noise around me. I saw no one but him.

But the voice in my head was loud and clear, too, reminding me of a question that burned inside: *Does he have something or not?*

As the night moved on, the shit bugged me more. Worse than the is-he-or-is-he-not-on-the-down-low game show in my head. I mean, of all the reasons why he kept me at arm's length, this made the most sense. I thought I'd finally solved the mystery, but had no idea how I wanted to approach the situation so we could work it out and get on with our lives together.

Unfortunately, my realization did nothing to calm my hormones, especially after watching the movie. Damn. Some *9 1/2 weeks* slash *Fatal Attraction* freaky-deaky booty-bumpin' goin' on up in there. I thought I was going to melt in my seat like the butter all over my popcorn. Lawd.

Got to my front door a little after midnight, my heart clobbering away. The rattle within me threatened to make a sista come undone. So many unanswered questions damn near set my head ablaze. I couldn't take it anymore. I had to know the deal.

"Well, babe, I guess I'm gonna call it a night. It's been cool—"

I snapped. "What the hell you mean you gonna 'call it a night'? Uh-uh, you ain't goin' no where."

Can you believe that fool started to walk away? He said, "Naw, babe, I gotta—"

"Boy, if you don't get yo' ass over here!"

Daryl froze. He turned to me, face on pause. Looked like he couldn't figure out how his lips worked.

That shit pissed me off, so a sista got ghetto. Fuck the neighbors.

"Damn, baby," he said, stepping back up the stairs, laughing. "Calm down. I was just playin'. I wouldn't dip out on you like that."

I jabbed the key in the lock. "Daryl, we need to talk. Now."

"Okay, Linda Blair," he replied, palms in the air. "Just don't twist your head around."

Yeah, whatever. That little shot at comedy didn't work.

We walked in and I flicked on one of my lamps, shedding a soft, orange glow throughout the room. African Musk incense still lingered, a fragrance designed to set a mood. For the first time tonight, I wondered if it would all go to waste.

I grabbed Daryl's hand and led him to the couch. Daryl sat down, but I stood, sucking in a vacuum of air to smother the heat churning up from my belly. I was ready to erupt on his ass, but had calmed down a little when I remembered the possible root to our dilemma.

"Baby, I need—"

"Hold on a second," I said, my palm braking whatever he had to say. I sat down, knotting his fingers in mine. "First, let me apologize for going off on you. That was wrong. But before I say anything else, I just wanna let you know that" —I took in another breath— "that whatever it is you might have it's ... it's okay. We can work around—"

"Huh?" he said, frowning. "What are you talking about?"

I swallowed. "You know, if you have a ... an STD, it's—"

"What? I don't have an STD! Where the hell you get that from?"

My jaw dropped. "You don't? I just assumed—"

"No, no, no." He chuckled, shaking his head. "Baby, I'm Grade A clean. What, you need proof? I've got all my paperwork."

My shoulders collapsed, lungs draining big gusts of air. "No, I believe you." I leaned against the armrest. "Wooo! Boy, you just don't know how happy I am to hear you say that! But how come every time we're together you always go back to your apartment without even trying to get some—"

"Shhhhhh," he commanded, a finger pressed to my lips. "Baby, I apologize. I do owe you an explanation about my, uh, situation. But I promise, soon it will all be clear. I actually have a little surprise for you, but I'm not quite ready to tell you about it yet. Still trying to finalize the plans."

My eyeballs swelled while I tried to suppress a monster smile. "Surprise? Well, why can't you tell me now?"

He shook his head. "I just gotta get a few things together. But for now," he said, as he stood up and stretched, "I'm gonna leave. I'll tell you more about the surprise tomorrow night. That cool?"

I looked up at him, pouting. *Here we go again.* "Um, okay," I said, sighing.

As he stretched, hands above his head, I stared at his crotch. Yum. The main course. The naughty in me tried to take over and I flashed him an evil grin. "Hey, babe, you sure you don't want me to..."

You woulda thought I was about to bite it off the way he dropped his hands between his legs so fast, covering the hot spot. "No, no! Um, we'll talk tomorrow, all right?" He adjusted his pants. "And trust me, you'll like the surprise, okay?"

Damn! I felt defeated, so I gave up the fight. He obviously didn't want a little "oral communication," either.

Collapsing my shoulders, I said, "That's fine, I guess."

We hugged and kissed, then he disappeared into the night like a fuckin' black Batman or some shit. Left me alone with me and my thoughts *again.*

I retreated to my bedroom. Flipping on the TV, I disrobed from yet another superwoman costume that didn't work on Daryl's Coochie Force Field and curled up in the bed. Now I had something new to ask myself questions about. Like this surprise. A *surprise? Really?* Don't get me wrong, I love surprises, but Daryl already had one huge question mark over his head and he just added to it. How you gonna drop bombs like that and leave me hanging? The man was a tease! I thought only women pulled these games!

Although frustrated, Daryl said he would tell me tomorrow night, so I left it at that—but my mind didn't.

Why couldn't he just tell me now? And what the fuck is his 'situation'?

Chapter 14

It actually came to me in the middle of the night.

I'd fallen asleep and of course, the sexual tension carried over into my subconciousness where Mr. Sandman took over and I'm telling you—he was 'bout to direct an epic big bang of a dream, *literally*. Daryl and I were co-stars in my own fantasy fuck-a-thon, and I knew I was fixin' to win Best Actress for my perfomance.

I don't know where the hell we were; I just know we were lying on a monster-sized bed. Daryl had taken his time undressing me. When he had a sista butt-ass naked, spread eagled on the bed, he traced his tongue between my thighs. To hell with that. I wanted him *inside* me.

"Baby, please," I begged. "Please put it in. I need to feel you. I want you to fuck me..."

He slid two fingers in. My moans grew louder, but I didn't want any damn fingers, either.

"No baby, just give it to me already. Give it *all* to me."

But then he said, "I want to, Michelle ... but ... I can't. Not right now. It won't listen to me."

I actually gave that fool the gas face in my dream, yelling, "What the fuck do you mean 'it won't listen to me?' "

Then I looked at it, all two or three inches of it. Soft. Wrinkled. Lookin' like a old-ass hairless cat. Fugliest thing I'd ever seen. I covered my mouth, backing up against the headboard. My dream had become a Stephen King nightmare.

I screamed, *"Nooooo! Can't be!"* It shriveled up, then disappeared inside a nappy crop of pubic hair the size of an Afro. *"Nooooo! It's limp dickkkkkk..."*

I awoke and sat straight up in bed, huffing and puffing. When I got my mental marbles in order, I cried, "That's *it!* Why didn't I think of that before?"

Guess my Daryl radar missed the big one; I don't know why it never occurred to me. I'd gone through all the "he's this or that" in my head—except one: What if Daryl wasn't trying to get it *in* because he couldn't get it *up*?

I shuddered at the thought. I'd heard and read about men having a permanent case of penis stage fright, but never met one before. Every man I'd known could supersize that thing within seconds. Dang, was it possible a man that fine could be impotent?

I admit, I knew nothing about erectile dysfunction. Yes, I'd seen the commercials for Viagra and all, but had no idea how it worked and if it worked on *every* man—or didn't work on some men at all. Maybe Daryl was one of those "some men."

I needed to research. Shit, I needed to talk to somebody about it, too. Too early for that, though, considering my nightstand clock said 4:37a.m. Still, I did a few Google searches before falling back asleep. Luckily, no more nightmares.

But later in the day, still itching for a phone call one-on-one, I decided to call my new girlfriend Tammy, who I met in school while pursuing her Masters. With our Texas roots and similar bumps in the road with men, we just hit it off. Last time I talked to her, she mentioned she was dating a doctor—and a black one at that!

I dialed her number. She answered on the second ring.

"Hey, Michelle! It's been a minute!"

"Hey Tammy! Yes, it has. How you doin'?"

"I'm good. Just reading and relaxing, enjoying my Saturday morning."

I sat on the couch, crossing my legs. "Yeah, I'm chillaxin' a lil' bit, too. What 'cha reading?"

"This wild book called *One Blood*. It's pretty good. Terrell left it here."

One Blood? Funny, once I heard "blood," I thought of Daryl and his problem. According to my research, he wasn't getting enough blood in the penile pipes.

I decided not to beat around the bush. "Um, regarding Terrell ... I actually have a medical question. You said he's a doctor, right?"

"Well, an eye doctor. What's up? Maybe I can ask him later today."

I took a deep breath. "Well, I've been dating this great guy. I mean, Tammy, he's damn near perfect. Everything I've ever wanted in a man. But it's been six weeks and we still haven't done the 'damn thing', yet, you know what I'm sayin'?"

"Seriously?"

"Yes. I think he might be ... impotent."

"Really? You plan on talking ... wait, *six weeks?*"

"Yup."

"You guys haven't talked about this yet?"

I slumped against the armrest, sighing. "Nope."

"Why not? Girl, I can't believe you've gone this long without talking to him about it!"

"I know, I know. Crazy, huh? Part of me was going with the flow, I guess, just following the yellow brick road, wondering where it would lead."

"What, you were waiting to find the Wonderful Dick of Oz? C'mon, girl!"

I cracked up. "Yeah, I know, right? But a normal man would've made the first move by now. I can only assume he has a problem with, uh, 'lifting'. And honestly, I don't know *how* to bring it up. That's a big deal for a guy."

"Yeah, you're right. The male ego is attached to their dingdongs, so I can only imagine how hard it is to bring up that subject."

"I can *only* imagine how hard it is, too." We laughed.

"No, but for real," she continued, "you two need to get to the bottom of this. You really don't even know if that's the problem, either. *Communicate.* "

"I know. Well, he said he has a surprise for me tonight that will clear things up. I'm kinda anxious to hear what it is."

"Well, there you go. Perfect time to talk it out, then work it out. And I mean, *really* work it out. Wooo, six weeks without the good-good when you *have* a man? I feel for you, girl."

"And that's not including the three months without it before I met him. Unless you count my toy."

"That doesn't count! There's nothing like the real thing, I don't care what anybody says! I bet you have so much built up tension you about ready to ride that thing off to the moon, huh?"

"Yes, ma'am!" I said, laughing. "You're right, though. Well, we'll see how things go tonight. I'm itching to know this surprise. Got me all in suspense."

"Me too! But listen, you guys have been together for a while, so obviously he's into you. I'm sure everything will be fine. Hey, we should double date soon. I'd like to meet him."

"Good idea. I'll talk to him about that tonight before I rodeo his ass."

She laughed. "I hear you. And, hey, you can always use your mouth, too! You know CPR, right?"

"What, uh, Cock ... Penis ... Resuscitation? That CPR?"

"Yeah, that one!"

We laughed a little more, then chit-chatted about trivial stuff. Tammy said, "Hey, did you still want me to ask Terrell about it? He may not know, but—"

"No, no, it's okay. I guess I really just wanted to vent a little. Thanks, though."

After talking for another ten minutes or so, we said our see-you-laters and hung up.

Yeah, Tammy was right. Daryl and I did need to get to the bottom of this. It wasn't really about finding out what the hell was up just so I could fast-forward to some dick treatment—well ... then again it kinda *was*—but obviously he was keeping shit from me, ya know? And that's not okay.

All right, he said this surprise will clear things up. If it doesn't, I'm gettin' in his ass.

After my girl-talk with Tammy, I went on a cleaning spree—Cascading the dishes, Pine-Soling the kitchen, Ajaxing my bathroom,

Windexing mirrors, Pledging the furniture, etc. I scrubbed everything from the windows to the walls.

Good thing I only had in one earpiece from my iPod because I don't think I would've heard the knock on the door. When I looked through the peephole, I saw Daryl on the doorstep.

Shit. "Just a sec, babe."

I didn't want him to see me looking like a slob, wearing baggy sweatpants and a dirty tank top. I was a little sweaty, too, so I ran to the bedroom right quick, checked out ol' girl in the standup mirror and threw on a T shirt. Once I was okay, I ran back to the front door.

"Hey, babe," I said, holding the door open, my smile sky high. He was lookin' good as usual, wearing long shorts and a sleeveless shirt. "What are you doing here? I thought you was coming by later?"

"Hey, gorgeous. What took you so long? You had to stash ol' boy in the closet before opening the door?"

"No, silly. I just wanted to look halfway decent. Been doing a lot of cleaning."

"Well, you look beautiful as always. Can I come in?"

"Boy, you know you can come in! Stop playin'!"

He laughed, wrapped his arms around my body, and damn near liquefied me with a kiss. Before he stepped on the carpet, he took off his tennis shoes. At least I had his ass trained in something.

He said, "Babe, I felt kinda bad about how I left you last night."

"Well, what was so different, Daryl? This little routine of early nights between us has been on repeat."

"Yeah, I know," he said, as we sat on the couch. "But, I'm about to let you know what's up. I told you I had a surprise for you. Ready to hear it?"

I smiled. "Of course."

He scooted closer to me until our knees tapped. "Are you doing anything next weekend?"

I shook my head. "No plans."

"You ever been to Palm Springs?"

"A long time ago. Why?"

"Well, I was finally able to get a reservation for next weekend. The resort has been booked, but today I managed to get us up in there."

Took me a second, but I realized what he was asking me. "So, you want me to join you?"

He nodded.

I wanted to scream. My lips wobbled as I tried to hold back a wide grin.

"And I promise you, babe, I *promise* you, I will answer *all* your questions then. I just want to wait until the time is right. Can we wait another week?"

I was about to protest in my head, but he stole a peck. Damn. A chill rippled through my belly, down to my thighs. My mouth was open, but the function that constructed spoken words had broken down.

"Can you go?"

I squeezed his hand. Somehow, I kept myself from jumping up like the next contestant on *The Price is Right*. I just said, "Boy, what do you think?"

He stole another peck. "Good, good. Got it for Friday through Sunday. I figure we can leave after work."

"That sounds good. I'll start packing right now. I mean, I—"

"Michelle, baby, calm down!" he cried, trying not to laugh. He stroked my cheek. "It's for *next* weekend. After that, you won't have to wait any longer. I promise."

I could've died right there. That man said "*I won't have to wait any longer.*" Lawd. After hearing that, Daryl waltzed his sexy butt out the door to play ball with his boys, who he said were waiting in his Yukon. I let him go in peace without getting a "piece."

What? Oh, I know what I said, girl! *"I'm gonna get in his ass..."* Yes, you don't have to remind me.

But I was so happy my man had asked me out on a romantic weekend getaway that it blurred everything I felt earlier. I didn't want to go off on him, really. And why should I? A man had never planned a trip for me before. *Never.* I usually planned the trips and suggested where to go. It felt good to have the tables turned. So sweet of my baby to center his weekend around me.

Smiling, I got all warm inside. *And* it appeared he had this whole impotency thing under control, since he planned on "answering *all* my questions."

So damn it, I could wait.

But you know what?

They say be careful with what you wish for because you might just get it.

Damn, ain't that the truth.

Chapter 15

"That's all you're bringing?" Daryl asked as he surveyed my luggage—or lack of it.

"Yup," I said.

He grabbed my bag. "Thought you'd be bringing more stuff for some reason."

"I don't know why you thought that. What, you think since I'm female I gotta bring my whole closet everywhere I go?"

He smiled. "Yeah. Isn't that what you females do?"

"No, boy." I smacked his arm. "This female travels light. Besides, if you don't plan on wearing a lot of clothes, why bring a lot of bags?"

His face softened when I said that, and he averted his eyes. I noticed his lips inch up, but he didn't respond. Just to let him know my mind wasn't in the gutter, I added, "It's supposed to be over a hundred degrees in Palm Springs."

He closed the back of his Yukon. "Um hum. Right."

I walked to the passenger side and was about to pull the door handle when Daryl, being a supreme gentleman, grabbed my hand and opened the door for me. Girl, he made me all weak in the knees when he did stuff like that. He always catered to me, treating me like a woman should be treated. Like a queen. A goddess. Through Daryl, I learned chivalry *does* exist in the world.

He leaned toward me and placed his lips on mine. With our tongues massaging each other, he tried to pull away, but I pushed my head forward to absorb his juices.

"Baby," he said, his voice muffled, "we need to get going. It's ... it's going on ... five, now. We ... need to roll. Traffic."

I released his bottom lip. "All right, all right." We chuckled.

In the car, I got comfy and buckled my seatbelt. Considering it was close to five on Friday afternoon, we knew we would sit in some traffic. This time, though, it didn't bother me. Not with Daryl by my side. I could think of worse things than being in a confined space with my man.

Daryl pointed to a CD case beneath my seat and asked me to get a CD. I grabbed the case, pulled out a CD labeled *Old School R&B & Rap Hits*, and threw that thing in the player. The Yukon became a back-in-the-day party on four wheels.

We were bumpin'! I had that man cracking up when I snapped my fingers, gyrating my butt against the seat and what-not—reciting lyrics to The Get Fresh Crew's "The Show." After a heavy rotation of Guy, Jodeci and Heavy D, Daryl loosened up, too—bobbin' his head, tappin' the wheel, ya know, doing his thing to get deep in the groove. Couldn't wait for him to get deep in *my* groove.

After forty-five minutes of crawling, traffic split open around Escondido. Daryl lead-footed the gas pedal, imitating the racecar driver Dale Earnhardt Jr.

As I looked out the window, I took in the landscape as we passed. The California hills stood at least a mile high with its ranch-style homes on top, kissing a Hawaiian-ocean blue sky. Clouds were worlds apart. Another postcard SoCal summer day, the perfect start to the "freekend."

Cranking the volume up higher, I sat back and enjoyed the rest of the ride.

Four hours. That's how long it took to get there.

Long drives definitely ain't the move for me, even with Daryl at the wheel. Believe me I tried, but my eyes weren't cooperating.

I did my best to take in the sights. Palm Springs looked like a trendy little community. We crept down Palm Canyon Drive, watching a gang of Palm Springers out and about. I noticed a runway of palm trees with snake-like light sabers of different colors wrapped around the trunks. They lit up the whole street—and it wasn't even Christmas yet. Upscale art galleries, boutiques, restaurants and nightclubs lined the block.

Seemed like all the action was within walking distance, but I didn't think I could make it. I yawned so much I thought I'd crack my jaw.

Daryl turned left on Tahquitz Canyon Way. "You tired?"

I scratched the corner of my eye. "No, no. I'm fine."

"You ain't got to lie. I saw you strugglin' the past hour or so. We don't have to do anything tonight. We can get some food and bring it back to the room."

I liked that idea, but at the same time, I felt if we didn't do anything, I'd be wasting our time away together.

"No, I'm fine." Said that in the middle of a yawn. "We can walk around, check out the town."

He made another left. Once I saw where we were staying, I perked up a little. "This is nice! I've never been to a Hilton Resort."

He cracked a slick grin. "Oh, yeah. That's how I roll. Only the best."

Girl! Now this is what I call a vacation! My Friday night definitely jumped off the right way. He pulled up in front and I was about to open the door, but he stopped me. Instead, he stepped out, walked around the front and opened the door for me, grinning and stuff.

"After you, Ms. Larsen," he said while holding my hand.

I smiled. "Thank you, babe."

Awww, Daryl. I wasn't "waiting to exhale" anymore, I can tell you that.

I stretched until my bones rattled. The warmth in the air surprised me. I thought it would be cool outside.

After we unloaded our bags, Daryl gave the young brotha in the cute valet suit a twenty-dollar tip and the keys. Had that boy's smile splittin' his whole grill.

After we checked in, we made our way to the third floor. Sleepy brain cells slapped me again as we stood in the elevator, my head leaned all up on Daryl's shoulder, just strugglin' to stay conscious.

Took us a little while to navigate the maze that led to our room. Once we found it, Daryl said, "Here we go, our own executive suite for two nights."

When he flipped on the lights, my bottom lip damn near bounced off the carpet. Very nice! Like a damn upscale condo and shit. Spacious living room with a couch and large, exotic plants. Fireplace. Cute kitchenette and ... awwwww watch out, now! A balcony overlooking the pool!

Of course, one amenity in particular made my body tingle: *One* large bedroom with *one* king-sized bed. That was all I needed to see.

We hadn't discussed sleeping arrangements, but I gave him a big hint after we dropped our bags on the bed. While he fumbled with the TV remote, flipping through the channels, I unpacked. I slid over to the dresser and put my stuff in one of the drawers.

He stopped on ESPN. Looking over at me, he said, "Wow, you settled in quick."

"Yep." All part of my plan to establish turf, dag-nabbit.

"I heard that. So what's the plan, Ms. Larsen? We ordering in or going out?"

I took in a deep breath, trying to catch my second wind. The bed looked good as hell, but my stomach didn't want to hear it. And I didn't think room service would cut it, so I grabbed my purse and said, "You know what? Let's go out. We can always order room service for breakfast."

He licked his lips. "Mmmm, breakfast in bed."

I smiled. It took every ounce of self-control not to rip off his clothes right then and there. But I held back. Needed some food in my pissed off belly to get my energy up. Besides, we had all night, and I *thought* it would be a long one.

We walked down the street at a snail's pace hand-in-hand, taking in the sights of the main drag Palm Canyon drive. Daryl bought us a couple of smoothies to settle our bellies a little, so we didn't eat right away. Then we dipped in and out of a few stores, stopped at the casino for little while, played a few slots, and lost some money. Palm Springs kinda reminded me of a miniature version of Hollywood Boulevard, especially with the little Walk of Fame thingy on the sidewalks. The woman at the front desk called it the "heart of a semi-tropical paradise."

That sounded perfect to me. I definitely felt like my heart lived in paradise.

I really don't know. Something pulsed within me ... a level of comfort ... sense of security ... but I couldn't put my finger on this new sensation's source. Whenever Daryl would place his arm around me and pull me close, tiny sparks would ricochet from my belly to my chest. Then they would grow, blending with the lust I'd somehow managed to suppress. I'd smile for no reason ... felt warmth spreading against my torso ... not like the desert air against my skin, but warm from the inside out. All I know is, while by his side, I never wanted to break away.

We did the tourist thing for about an hour or so. I noticed Daryl getting his yawn on, too.

I said, "Now you gettin' tired, huh?"

"Yup. Wanna get something to eat and roll back to the room? Stomach's growling like it's mad at the world, now."

I stroked my belly. "That's fine. Mine is, too."

We found a Mexican food spot, ordered two chimichangas to go, then headed back to the room.

Man, I was *drained*. It's funny, after weeks of my hungry body yearning for my first night with Daryl, a bump-and-grind finale was the last thing on mind. All I wanted was some horizontal peace and at least eight hours of rapid eye movement. I'd need *all* my energy when it came time for the freaky-deaky crowning glory.

Got back to our room around eleven o'clock, but it felt like two in the morning. Daryl flipped on the TV and I laid out the food on the bed. It was like a picnic in the middle of our California King.

We got our eat on. I was so hungry I had to remind myself to chew.

Daryl said, "Are you having fun so far, Ms. Larsen?"

I swallowed some Sprite. "More fun than you know. Just wish I wasn't so tired."

"Don't be." He yawned. "I'm pretty tired myself. We have all day tomorrow to do the fun stuff."

"It's gonna be pretty hot. Do you want to get in the pool?"

When I asked that, his face cracked like I cussed him. He twisted his lips and lines in his forehead appeared. "Um ... maybe."

"Maybe? Don't you want me to show off my new bikini?"

He shifted his eyes to the TV. "Uh, we'll see. I'm not much of a swimmer."

"Ooookay."

I let it go. Yeah, that ticked me off a bit, but no need to start a petty argument while on vacation.

Turning to the TV, I noticed one of those "male enhancement" commercials. Perfect timing. Soon as the narrator said something about "extending your manhood," Daryl flipped the channel.

I noticed Daryl's expression. He looked a little ticked off, too, like the commercial had something to do with it. That was my cue to break the ice.

I was just about to ease into the impotency conversation when out of nowhere, he said, "You know what? We don't have any bottled water. I need my water in the morning."

My forehead wrinkled up. "Ummmm, right. I'm sure we can order some up."

He stood and grabbed his food container. "Actually, I think I'm gonna run to the store and pick up a few things. You need anything besides Riesling?" He winked.

"Ha Ha. No, I'm okay. Soooo, you're not going to finish eating?"

He shook his head. "Naw. I've had enough for now, so I'll put this in the fridge. Wanna get there before they close."

"Well let me go with you." I put my fork down.

"Naw, you stay here and rest. I'll be back before you know it." And that was it. He was gone.

Damn. Guess I'll have to wait to talk about it when he gets back.

His abrupt exit killed the rest of my appetite. I cleared off the bed and got comfortable. *Too* comfortable, actually. Don't know how long I was staring at the TV, but it didn't take long for it to stare at *me*. Once my eyelids dropped, the lights went out. Couldn't fight it anymore; the sandman doubled-decked my butt into the underworld.

Next thing I knew, I was wiping spit from the side of my face and flapping my eyelids, trying to clear my vision in a dark room. My mind didn't register the surroundings at first, but as soon as I saw the dresser and the window, I remembered where I was.

I sat up, scooted to the edge of the bed and stretched my arms high. Clock on the nightstand read 2:43am.

"Damn," I said. "I was *out.*"

I frowned when I noticed the TV. Didn't remember turning it off, either. "Where is Daryl?"

I rewound to just before I went to sleep: *He went to the store ... I fell asleep ... and ... and he should be here!* Walking out of the room, swerving my head back and forth, I searched for the light switch. A soft glow sliced the darkness through a window by the couch. I looked down, then smiled at the two large feet propped up on the armrest.

Easing a small sigh of relief, I whispered, "*Look at him. Sleeping like a baby.*"

I tiptoed to the end of the couch and knelt down, setting my face a few inches from his head. He looked so peaceful; he even hummed when he breathed. What a beautiful thing to witness: my man in his most vulnerable state.

I traced my index finger around his lips, felt the smooth texture of his thin mustache. Then I mapped a line across his cheek to his jaw. Skin so Noxzema soft, not a razor bump anywhere. As I made my way to the other side of his face, he shifted. Raising my finger, I sat still. His eyes never opened.

The last thing I wanted was to disturb him while sleeping, but he just looked so damn edible laying there like that, all helpless and stuff. The naughty vibes I'd been suppressing stirred again and the only thing standing between us was that damn blanket.

I thought, *I could slide under the blanket with him, then slide him out of his pants and...*

But I couldn't do it, especially since he had impotency issues. We needed to talk it out first; I just didn't know how to open up that can of worms yet. But mark my words, we would not be leaving Palm Springs without getting to the bottom of our non-existent sex life. I could only imagine his discomfort about the problem, but once everything was out in the open, I was convinced a few Viagra pills would get the party started, especially after reading about the power of the magic blue pill during my research. And best believe I had a few of 'em in my bag.

Besides, making love is a two-way street, you know, and I needed his full and conscious participation. Shoot, I didn't want to resort to desperate measures, jacking him for a little nookie while he slept and shit. I could wait a little longer. Hell, I waited this long.

I kissed his forehead. Without thinking, I said, "I love you."

Wow. *Wow.*

I hadn't said those words in I don't know how long, but they flowed out of me so naturally. No, it wasn't about belly-smackin' lust anymore. My heart, brain, and gut were all in harmony, and I realized what I felt was so much deeper than a few much-needed Daryl-induced orgasms.

I not only loved him, I was *in* love with him. No man had every made me feel the way he did.

But I knew once we *finally* crossed that bridge? Wooo, *man.* I anticipated fireworks, explosions, combustion—maybe even a few broken bones, dag-nabbit.

I shivered. Hell, I almost felt sorry for him. Making love is fine and all, but I knew once we got into it, I was going to bull-ride his ass into next week and leave more than enough scratches to mark my territory. Maybe even a few bite marks.

"Rest up, baby, I whispered, *"Tomorrow night your beautiful, brown ass is mine."*

Chapter 16

Sunlight streaked through the crack in the window. I rolled over and saw the other pillow, a little disappointed to not have Daryl's warm body blessing the other half of the bed. For some reason, I thought he had gotten up from the couch and eased under the sheets next to me. Didn't happen. Maybe I was dreaming. Oh well.

I didn't want to rush him with a flood of morning bacterial funk, so I stepped into the bathroom, brushed my teeth and knocked back a capful of Listerine. I washed my face and wiped the crud out the corners of my eye. After one last once-over, I stepped out to find my morning chocolate delight.

Apparently, chocolate delight had other plans. The blanket was folded neatly on the couch, but Daryl apparently got ghost.

I scanned the room, my forehead wrinkled. "Where is that man, now?"

The sound of water froze me. *What the hell?*

I could hear it nearby, but couldn't tell from where exactly. I turned to a door on the opposite side of the living room.

Hmmmm.

As I approached the door, the sounds grew louder. My eyebrows danced and crumpled around my forehead. *Did a damn pipe burst up in here?*

I nudged the door open. I poked my head inside, then jerked back, eyes wide. *Well, I'll be damned.*

A small office. Pretty cool. This whole time I thought it was a closet.

Damn, this whole place was bigger than my apartment! I ran my hands across the mahogany desk and noticed he left his laptop open connected to the Internet with his Facebook page up. Oh, he shouldn't have done that! I tapped my lip, staring at his chocolate head in the profile box, then noticed he had new messages.

Oh, hear we go. Should I?

I didn't ask myself a second time.

As I settled into the plush leather chair, I clicked on the inbox. That's when I noticed another door to my right *and* the source of the running water. Obviously a bathroom with a shower ... where Daryl stood behind it ... butt ass naked.

I swallowed. *Shit.*

My heartbeats sped up, face all flushed. I couldn't tell if the sudden rise in my body temperature stemmed from me clicking on Daryl's private messages behind his back—or that I had a chance to enact my own wet porno flick.

As dumb as it sounds, curiosity killed the kitty cat. At least for a second.

Girl, I know it was wrong, but how could I *not* look? You can tell a lot about a man from his email, you know. That's how I caught my ex cheating.

My initial scan of his inbox didn't raise any red flags. No stray females at all, and most of the messages were to yours truly. In fact, I even found a message to some other guy, a friend from another state. Daryl was raving about—and these are his words—"the beautiful new lady in his life" that lived in his complex. Damn, called me "beautiful" in a written message to one of his boys. He even mentioned my name, girl.

I covered my mouth, blushing until my cheeks looked like the shades of an apple, I'm sure. Every time I tried to dig up dirt, Daryl came up smelling like roses. I needed to just accept Mr. Wonderful *as* wonderful and stop looking for skeletons in the closet.

A heavy dose of good sense kicked in, as well as a little bit of panic for snooping, so I placed everything back how I found it. I had new matters to handle, like making my porno debut with Daryl. I thought about running back to the drawer where I stashed the blue pills, but decided against it. I figured I could teach Daryl my own version of CPR first.

As I got closer, I could hear him singing. Placing my ear against the door, I dropped my jaw, covering my mouth to muffle the laughter.

"Is this boy singing Justin Bieber?"

Yes, he was! So cute, too! Grown ass man singing a teenybopper song!

I tried to open the door, but it was locked, so I tapped on it. "Hey, babe, you want some company?"

I was just about the slither out of my shorts when the water cut off! I heard the shower curtain push back when he said, "Oh! Uh ... I'm done, babe. I have my clothes in here, too, so I'll be dressed and ready to go for breakfast soon. How 'bout a raincheck on that shower?"

My head dropped to the side as if a weight pulled it down. Ugh!

Shaking my head, I stared at the door, twisting my lips trying to figure if I should get ghetto or just back off. After about ten seconds of a back-and-forth between myself and I, I eventually said, "fine" and got up outta up there.

Back in the bedroom, I had to yank in a few large breaths to calm Queen Bitch emerging within me, so to avoid going off on Daryl, I grabbed my clothes, went into the bathroom, locked the door and took my own damn shower. Alone. *And* a cold one at yet.

When I finished, I got dressed in the bathroom. If Daryl could play that game, so could I. I needed a few moments to myself 'cause I was still a little ticked off, anyway.

But I didn't want to stay pissed, especially at the start of our first Saturday morning on a sunny Palm Springs day, ya know? Staring at the slightly fogged up mirror, I whispered, *"All right, Michelle, calm down, now. It's okay. Besides he planned this whole trip for us, so no need to get bent outta shape. We'll have plenty of time to 'get wet' together."*

I heard Daryl turn on the TV. Once I got myself together, I opened the door. Man. Slowing my roll, I leaned against the doorway, crossing my arms, just smiling. What a *view*. Daryl was lathering himself up with lotion, wearing shorts and a tank top. We damn near matched, colors and everything. Soon as I saw him rubbing up and down his biceps, the last remnants of Queen Bitch went beddy-bye.

"Mornin', gorgeous," he said, pearly whites gleaming. "How'd you sleep?"

"Pretty good. Was hoping you would've come into bed. How was the couch?"

"It was cool. You was sprawled out on the bed, so I let Sleeping Beauty get her beauty sleep. I went to the couch and got on the Internet for a while before I passed out."

On the tube, the newscaster said sumn' 'bout ninety-two degrees outside. Shoot, that's desert heat for yo' ass—enough to make a sista burnt-toast black.

I walked over to him and gave him a peck. He said, "You ready to get our eat on and do some fun stuff?"

I nodded. "Yes. And oh, nice Justin Bieber imitation."

His eyeballs damn near poked all the way out. "You weren't supposed to hear that!"

We laughed and carried on to the next adventure.

I scooped up a few brochures from the lobby and we grabbed a table in the hotel restaurant. After studying the brochures, I suggested a nature walk. Daryl looked at me like I lost half my grey matter.

"You're tryin' to hike in this heat?"

"Well, it says right here the canyon trails have plenty of trees and shade. It would be nice to see some waterfalls and stuff. Besides, we would get some exercise, too. You know we always trying to work on our fitness."

That fitness comment sealed the deal. Daryl and I pretty much obliterated breakfast, then headed out to the Indian Canyons. After loading up a backpack with bottled water, we enjoyed a leisurely hike on a few trails, strolling along streams of water with rocky desert hills as our backdrop. Beautiful slices of God's work were all around us. Geez, I'd never seen so many different species of plants in my life. Straight out of Jurassic Park or sumn', like if I touched them, I'd either get swallowed up or injected with poison. It was so peaceful, though. Reminded me why I loved California so much.

141

By noon, the desert sun wasn't holdin' nothin' back, hurling heat waves all up in our faces. No problem for me, though. Sistas can get their sweat on, too.

Somehow it turned into a competition thing between Daryl and me 'cause he'd been teasing me, talkin' 'bout how I wouldn't be able to keep up with him and stuff. Whateva. He ain't said nothin' but a word. With my backpack and Timberland boots, I hiked them trails like I had a permanent residence up in that place.

After about an hour of the sun pile-driving heat rays on us, Daryl tried to be slick. He kept complaining about having to use the bathroom and what not. Yeah, right. Such a big baby. I'd noticed he was limping a little, but I waved it off as a front. Me? I was fine. As long as I wore sunglasses, downed massive amounts of H20 and got my five-minute dose of shade under a big ass tree, I was cool. He couldn't hang with *me*. You know I had to ride him for that.

We got back in the Yukon and hit the road. Next on my to-do list was the Palm Springs Tram trip to Mount San Jacinto. We turned on Tramway Road and zigzagged three miles up a steep hill to park. Loved the spontaneity we had. No plans—just see it, then do it.

Great view from the tram. You'd hear all kinds of "ooohs" and "aaahhhs" from folks pointing at the mountains and Chino Canyon. But I ain't gonna lie, I had to padlock myself around Daryl's arm. As we waved goodbye to level ground, the passenger "bucket" we stood in sped up the mountain, suspended from a thick, metal cable. That thing would rock and my heart would drop. When I got the nerve I would take a quick photo, then latch back onto him. Daryl would laugh, but comforted me with hugs and forehead kisses.

I let out a breath when we docked at the Mountain Station about fifteen minutes later. The tram doors opened and to my surprise, icy air rushed me. I felt like I had left summer and stepped into winter. Man, I needed that cold breeze.

Mountain Station was a three-story structure with gift shops, dining facilities, observation areas—the whole nine. Lawd, the scene in front of us was *bea-u-ti-ful*. Endless blankets of forest green lay before my eyes, the wilderness in its purest state. Enough to take your breath away.

Daryl tapped my shoulder. "Look."

I gasped. Lawd, what a phenomenal aerial view of Palm Springs. I crossed my arms, stood back, and gazed at the endless desert scene. Damn.

Then I heard a loud rustle. I whipped around and saw five horses high-stepping to a stop. Horseys! Girl, I was giddy. Started clapping, jumping up and down, grabbing Daryl's arm.

"Look, baby," I said, acting all goofy, "they have horses! Wanna ride the horsey?"

Daryl rolled his head away. "Um ... aren't you getting hungry? Let's go eat and—"

I smacked my tongue. "C'mon, Daryl. I know you didn't come all the way up here just to eat. Let's ride, you big baby."

He scratched his neck, then sucked his teeth. What the hell was that about? I didn't understand the big deal. *Damn, do horses scare him?*

A couple strolled by us with two pre-teen boys charging in front. The man gave the horse handler two fives. With the handler's help, the super-happy boys hopped on and locked their small fingers around their horse's reins, looking like twin blazing saddles.

I nudged Daryl with my elbow. "Now if two boys barely in puberty can ride, you can, too."

An older woman in front of us laughed. Daryl narrowed his eyelids at me.

I showed my palms. "All right, all right. We don't have—"

"So, you really want to ride, huh?"

I cried, "Yes! Pleeeease?" Like a little girl, I batted my eyelashes.

He stroked his chin and then said, "Okay. You ride the dark brown one; I'll ride this gray one behind it."

Riding the "dark brown one" sounded good to me. After doin' my silly happy dance, we maneuvered around piles of horse doodoo and Daryl gave the handler two fives. After a little demonstration on how to mount, the handler helped me place my foot in the stirrup. Took me a couple of tries, but I finally swung my leg up. Once I grabbed the reins, shoot, you couldn't tell me nothin'. All I needed was some boots and a cowboy hat.

Daryl was already on his horse. His daddy long legs made it easy. Sittin' up there winking at me. Punk.

Once the handler mounted the horse in front, away we went.

We slow-galloped down narrow dirt trails underneath monster-sized trees. I closed my eyes, breathing in the mountain air that swiped my face. Ahhhh. So fresh. So clean.

I'll tell you what, though—the slow up-and-down motion of the stallion between my legs set fire to my imagination. Shoot, I had to open my eyes before I got too excited, ya know? Ha!

We stopped a few times so the handler could do his Mount San Jacinto history spiel. I had the pleasure of watching the horse in front of me flip his tail and drop boulder-sized doodoo to the ground. Nasty.

When I turned to check on Daryl, I frowned. That boy was wiping his forehead with the back of his hand. Looked like he would pass out any minute.

I said, "Daryl, you okay?"

He shook. "Huh? Oh, yeah."

"You sure?"

"Yeah ... I'm cool."

I stared for a second, then turned around. *Damn, I hope he don't fall out on me*, I thought. For the rest of the trip, I kept checking on him. He was all smiles whenever I turned around, but I could tell homeboy wanted to get the hell off that horse.

When we finished our little joy ride, Daryl hopped off before the handler. He limped toward me and helped me down.

"Are you sure you're alright?" I asked. He looked like he was in pain.

"Oh, yeah, yeah. I'm fine." He stretched out his back. "So, you ready to eat? The restaurant here is supposed to be the best in Palm Springs."

"Yes. Let's go." We headed back to Mountain Station, found a restaurant, and sat at a table on the patio so we could enjoy the scenic views of the Sonoran Desert while we got our grub on. One of the most romantic meals of my life.

With my belly full of barbecue beef ribs and vegetables, I was ready for a nappy nap, so we made our way back to the room to crash. I needed to get horizontal for a good two, three hours to prepare for the full night ahead.

Good thing I took that nap.

Chapter 17

"What's up, babe? You 'bout ready to go to the casino with yo' sexy self?"

I looked up and saw Daryl standing in the doorway wearing a short-sleeve button down shirt and chino pants, shooting straight up the fine-o-meter once again.

"Hold on one second." I stood and did a final once-over in the mirror. I rocked a casual look—V-neck blouse, heeled sandals, shorts nice and snug—the curve in my thick booty cheeks like a lower-case letter "b". It didn't take long to realize Daryl had told the truth about a sista.

I grabbed my purse off the dresser. "Okay. My sexy self is ready." Daryl chuckled.

We left the hotel. On foot, it took us five minutes to get to the casino. My stomach growled like the Lion King, so we hit the Aqua Bar and Grill near the casino. We ate outside, soaking in the night desert air as we laughed and conversed. I got lost in his smile, seduced by the rhythm of his bass-filled voice. I swear, I couldn't think of anywhere else I wanted to be.

The mood was perfect.

As the wine flowed, naughty cravings bloomed. At least ... they bloomed for *me*. Wasn't long before my primal urges morphed into something wicked ... dirty ... shoot, dare I say *barbaric*. Didn't plan on suppressing my True Blood hunger for flesh anymore. I'd been doing that for too damn long. *No more.* Tonight, Daryl was gonna have to come correct after popping a few doses of Viagra.

Emphasis on "come."

Steak and lobster hit the spot. After sharing a slice of cheesecake for dessert, we left the restaurant and wandered over to the casino, heading straight to the slot machines. I did my thing on a Wheel of Fortune slot. If I could just end the night with a picture of me holding a five-figure cardboard check, I'd be all right. You know how it goes, though—ya win a little bit, ya get all happy, then lose it all ... and then some.

Shoot. Something about losin' money makes you wanna get yo' drink on, ya know? I waved at an older waitress in a tacky miniskirt. Poor thing. That ancient heifer knew good and well she had no business wearing that skirt. And with fishnet panty hose and circus clown make-up? Puh-lease.

She walked up to us and asked for our orders. At the same time, Daryl and I said, "Long Island, please."

We looked at each other and smiled. We were in sync. *Connected.* We just needed to "connect" on another level.

Despite my losses, we had a good time. Just smiling, rooting for each other, gettin' our drink on, cursing at the machines, ya know. But after another round of Long Islands, liquid sin must've pilfered a route to my brain 'cause a sista got a little woozy-wobbly. My brain cells were playing hopscotch inside a hormonal blaze. Damn. So hot. Ready for action, you hear me? Fire tortured my body from the inside. I damn sure wasn't focused on no slot machines anymore.

Daryl tapped my shoulder. "You getting bored?"

I sighed. "Just getting tired of losing. Feeling a little tipsy, too."

To my surprise, he said, "We can leave if you want after I lose my twenty. Maybe hit up a club or sumn'."

No, I don't want to do that, I thought. But my mouth said, "That's fine."

"Hmmm, you don't sound very enthused," he said. "You want to do something else? We can go back to the room instead, maybe watch a pay-per view? We had a long day today—I wouldn't mind a little R and R. I'm down either way."

Thank you, I thought. And yet, I didn't want to be the party pooper. After all, we were still on vacation and leaving the next day, so to be neutral, I said, "Let's just see what happens when we leave here. We'll work it out."

He smiled. "That's cool. "

I waited for Daryl to gamble away his last twenty dollars. As he pushed the machine button, I fell into a little trance 'cause he was pushing *my* buttons, too. I became lost, zeroed in solely on Daryl Almighty. *Especially* that bald head of his. Smooth as a marble. *Flawless.* So perfect. So round. So...

Damn. Those Long Islands concocted some crazy fantasies, boy. Buzz had my brain in a cloud. I conjured up some wild stuff involving my tongue and his head:

Mmm ... I love the shape of that thing. I just want to stroke it ... rub it down ... like a genie lamp. Damn, it kinda looks like a nice, round milk dud, actually. I love me some milk duds, too. Delicious. Hmmmmmmmmmm. I bet if I lick his scalp right now he'll even taste—

"Michelle!"

I shook. His voice kicked me out of La La land. If he hadn't said anything, I probably *would* have licked his head.

I replied, "Huh? What?"

He smiled, giving me the side eye. "Are you staring at me?"

Embarrassed, I tried to play it off. "Oh no," I started, "I was just daydreaming about..." But then I paused.

Time to put an end to my good girl role, damn it. No more games and no more holding back. Daryl the Boy Scout needs to know the real deal.

"I was just daydreaming about what you will feel like inside of me." I dropped my voice. "I can't wait to find out."

He stopped, then looked around. I could tell my words sparked something inside him, made his face twist from surprise.

But he didn't turn away. Instead, he curved his lips upward. A naughty glint flickered in his eyes. Homeboy knew the deal.

He leaned toward me. "Well, Ms. Larsen," he said, his voice dropping an octave or two. "Let's go back to the room so I can show you what I feel like. You've waited long enough."

Aw shit!

Fi-na-ly! He planted a soft, sweet peck on me. Our lips danced, his eyes teased.

I almost fell out my chair.

From that moment, I switched priorities quick. Nothing else mattered 'cause when he laid those juicy lips on me? Wooooo! Forget the casino! Destination: King-size bed! Shoot, I was ready to do some supersonic, junglistic, Matrix-type fuckin'. I ain't lyin. The kind where you wake up in the morning and see sheets all over the floor, scratches on the wall, mattress halfway on, window curtains all lopsided. Like a tornado ran through that place, shit.

We high-tailed it outside. I took his hand in mine, pulling him as hard as I could. My heels clicked against the sidewalk, damn near scorching the cement. Considering my buzz, I'm surprised my ass could walk as fast as I did.

"Slow down, girl!" he said, laughing.

"Hells no! You need to keep up."

I wasn't playin', either. I was truckin'. Couldn't wait to smack his flesh against mine. I didn't want to have sex, make love, screw—none of that soft stuff. I wanted to get *fucked. Hard.* And you know what I'm talkin' 'bout; don't play stupid, now. Hair pulling, ass slapping, loud hyena-like shrieks. Damn. The way I felt, I was willing to risk a twisted spine, too.

I barely remember our walk back to the room, but I know by the time he opened the door it was on. You don't hear me, girl. I'm talkin' sloppy, deep throat kisses as if we were filming scenes for Basic Instinct 4. Nothing in our path was safe. Ka-klunk, blam, thump! Just banging against furniture and knocking stuff over like we ain't been house-trained!

We somehow made it to the bedroom. I clawed at his shirt and ran my hands down his chest to get to his pants. That's when he tensed up and backed away.

"Chelle, chill out!"

"Chill? Uh-uh," I said, panting. "You done started some shit, now!"

I wanted to get this party started right! I stepped toward him, reached down and tried to touch between his legs. He grabbed my hand and pushed me back.

"Michelle! Stop now!"

What? No! Not again!

I almost called that fool out his name. My chest heaved from the sudden rush of oxygen through my mouth.

"What?" I screamed, gasping. "Why do you keep stopping me?"

He held my hand. "Sit down for a second. We need to talk. I need to prepare you for this."

What the hell? I sat on the edge of the bed. "Talk about what? Prepare me for what? *What?*"

Daryl took a deep breath, reached over to the light switch and flicked it on.

He said, "I need to ... my thing is ... damn."

I didn't have time for all that freakin' stuttering. "Look," I said, "you need to spit it out, okay? I'm tired of this beating around the bush bullshit 'cause yo' ass ain't tellin' me a damn thing and I'm gettin' all hot and bothered over this whole situation and I—"

"Michelle! Will you let me finish?"

I stopped my mile-a-minute motor mouth. Sucked in a long breath to calm myself.

Daryl lowered his head. For a few seconds, he didn't say a word. Finally he spoke. "I have a, uh, little problem."

Chapter 18

I rolled my eyes. "I should've known. Just my luck."

"What?"

I threw my hands up. "Another man with issues. Shit, I've jumped through enough hoops over your ass, too."

"Well, I highly doubt you've seen an issue like this. I want to make sure you can—"

"What, Daryl? What?" Then my eyes got wide. My jaw dropped. "Oh, no! You *do* have an STD, huh?"

"No! Not that. I—"

"Then you *are* impotent! Look, I've done some research and—"

"Michelle! Damn, woman, that's not it. I—"

"Then what is it? Are you gay? On the down-low? Married to Donald's mother?"

"No, no and *no!* I ... shoot." He looked to the floor. "You know what? Let me just freakin' show you."

"Show me? Show me what?"

"This."

He unbuttoned his shirt, slid it off and dropped it to the floor. After tugging on his zipper, he pushed his pants down to his ankles.

I swallowed.

Then I screamed.

Woo, doggie.

I rushed both hands to my mouth to stifle the noise. I'm lucky I don't have a weak heart. Goodness. My eyeballs almost catapulted from their sockets as drool formed in the corner of my lips.

Now, they say the earth has seven wonders. Well, that's a lie. I'm here to tell you Daryl has the eighth!

With his pants wrapped around his ankles, I saw it first-hand, the hard physical evidence on the scene. The eighth wonder ... right in that room!

This was the problem that he kept in hiding all this time? Wow, he hid that problem extremely well. I had no idea it could even *be* a problem.

If the *longest dick I'd ever seen in my life* is a "problem," damn, did I have the solution?

And that boy said "little" problem. Yeah, right. That thing was so damn long, I swear he could have tied that bitch in a knot. I'm not kidding, girl.

My eyes inched up. Daryl looked down with a half-grin. Had his hands on his hips, legs spread apart, standing like Long Dong Silver up in here.

Again I swallowed, my gaze moving back down. Could not believe what stood before me. Lawd.

"I've been wanting to share this with you," he said, "but I didn't want to just whip it out, ya know? Sorry I've acted so immature about this. I dig you a lot and ... well ... let's just say it's been a problem for me in the past."

My lips quivered, but I seized control of them. "I-I-I understand."

"I'm sure this answers your questions, right?"

I leaned forward, tilting my head a little. "Um ... ye-yeah."

Everything made sense now—the pimp limp, slick ways he covered his crotch, the loose pants, long shorts pass his kneecaps. And I understood why he didn't want to just "whip it out" as he said. Probably would've scared the shit out of me. Sheesh.

I blinked several times. Shoot, had to. That thing couldn't possibly be real. But do they even make prosthetic ding-dongs? "Wow," I said, still staring. "No wonder I've, uh, seen you scratching down there so much."

"Scratching?"

"Y-yeah. I noticed you dig your fingers between your legs a lot."

"What? Oh! Naw, naw, baby. I wasn't scratching. More like readjusting. Ol' boy gets outta position sometimes. Gets uncomfortable if I let him get all balled up."

Guess that made sense.

We sat quiet for a moment—him staring at me, me staring at Mr. Meat Combo Supreme.

After a short pause, I said, "Daryl?"

"Yeah?"

"H-how ... how long is it?"

"Eleven inches. When hard, closing on thirteen."

My bottom lip dropped at least another inch. For a second, I think blood flow to my brain shut down. Had to grip the end of the mattress to keep from sliding off the bed, still a little woozy. I mean, c'mon—eleven inches? Limp? Damn near thirteen when hard? Over a freakin' foot? That's an "a-dick-tion" for yo' ass!

I looked up. "Do you mind if I ... um ... can I just look at it for a while?"

He giggled. "Sure, go 'head. I'll be right here."

Have mercy. I had to get my senses straight. I rubbed my eyes. Blinked a few more times. It stayed there, like a dark-brown sleeping beauty.

For some reason, Lawrence popped in my head. Remember him? Shoot, Daryl was the anti-Lawrence. Comparing Lawrence's teenie weenie to Daryl's long schlong was like matching a tricycle against a Cadillac Escalade. I don't know about you, but I prefer the Caddy.

I stared at the base of Daryl's yardstick where his two "buddies" dangled, then my gaze tiptoed down the rest of the anaconda——not stopping until damn near *between his kneecaps*. I kid you not. It rested in a straight but limp position with its helmet pointing toward the floor. Looked like a dark sock filled with sand.

Girl, it got quiet *quick*. I fell into a soundproof vacuum, isolated from all that surrounded me. Everything around my line of sight went black, my vision glued to the most glorious piece of male flesh I'd ever seen. Nothing else was in that room except me, the "Dicktator," saliva that rolled off my bottom lip, and the "sweat" between my legs.

For a good ten seconds, something came over me. Can't explain it. One would only know if they experienced it first-hand, I guess. It was weird. *Very* weird. Felt like I'd kneeled before the presence of excellence ... or some masculine majesty that equaled that of a Roman Emperor. I'd become rapt in the royal glow of a real life King Dingaling!

Did I need to render honors or something? Damn, should I hand-salute, curtsy, kiss its crown like you kiss the hand of a mob boss—what? All I know is, I had hit the "blackpot". I almost cried. It was so wonderful.

I know, I know. I was trippin'. Tipsy, remember?

I raised my hand to touch it, curious, but cautious. Mind so foggy I almost convinced myself it would bite me.

I poked its head. It swayed back toward the dresser, then to me. I got all excited—I think I even clapped like a little girl. Deciding I was safe, I poked it harder. Again it swung backward, then landed in my palm. That thing gave me so much inebriated joy!

I leaned in closer, my nose barely an inch away. Saw the small ridges around its crown. A large snake-like vein ran down the middle. Didn't see no toes or a heel, so it wasn't a third leg—but damn close.

I didn't stop there, though. Dag-nabbit, I wasn't through with my "research."

I held it in my palm, stroking that puppy with my other hand. So smooth, warm—just like Daryl's face. I kept caressing it until I found the rock I'd longed for.

Seconds later, his jackhammer swelled under my fingers. Oh, boy! The blood rush came, and I'm surprised Daryl didn't pass out 'cause I'm damn sure that thing carried at least half his blood supply.

Then it lifted like a crane; thick and hard, the flesh damn near pushing my hand away! Shoot, it didn't take long for it to super-size from floppy to rocky. That thing poked its Darth Vader head right at me!

It stuck out like a diving board, so I tapped the "head" and watched it bob up and down. "Hee hee, haw haw!" I laughed, acting all goofy. "Boing! Boing! Boing! Look at it go! Look at it go!"

"Excuse me?"

I shuddered. That baritone voice damn near shook the piss out of me.

"Are you having fun?"

I finally broke from my King Dingaling trance. Bursting out in laughter, I covered my face with my hands. So silly of me—but I couldn't help it. That bat freakin' altered my brain cells and shit; yanked me from reality and slammed me headfirst into fantasy. Shoot, Daryl didn't even exist anymore; King Dingaling had become Superman and me Lois Lane.

I looked up at Daryl. He stared back with a silly grin.

"I have one question, Ms. Larsen."

"What's that?"

"Do you think you can handle this?"

His words vibrated in my head. *Do I think I can handle this?*

I stared back at King Dingaling, its head rigid, raw and right between my eyes. For a hot second, I thought a forked tongue would lick my face.

I tried to jump back into a somewhat rational state-of-mind, but my hormones spoke for me. I damn sure wasn't thinking straight 'cause I said, "Ummm ... yeah. Noooo problem."

"All righty, then." He pointed down. "There's a condom in my right pocket."

As I bent down to reach his pants, I bumped my forehead against *his* "head."

"Ow," I said, rubbing my noggin, trying not to laugh and what-not. Kinda stung a little, actually, being steel-hard and all. Luckily it didn't poke my eye out.

While covering my lips to keep from giggling, I dug into Daryl's pocket. That's when I noticed he wore no underwear.

I said, "You're not wearing any drawers."

"I know," he said. "Being this big, sometimes I have to, what we big boys call, 'freeball.' "

I nodded. Made perfect sense to me. Couldn't imagine that thing folded up in a pair of tighty whiteys.

Went back to the task at hand. Probably took less than five seconds to find the Trojan. Freak mode had kicked into fifth gear. Couldn't wait to slide the rubber over that brontosaurus' neck.

Before I ripped it open, I noticed the gold packet had black letters that said "for length and girth." Damn, condoms designed for King Dingalings? Who knew?

I tore that bitch open, pulled out the lubricated glove and rolled that bad boy on until it couldn't go any more. Did it nice ... smooth ... and slow. No need to rush anymore. The wait was over—I finally got my trophy.

To my surprise, the rubber rolled all the way down. Gave the "joystick" a glossy, silvery, steel look, like a sword. Damn, girl. My very own Lord of the "Dings," with Sir Dick-a-Lot standing over me.

Now, I know you don't want to hear about how that freak of nature fit in the condom, huh? You want to know how it fit in *me*, right?

Daryl hit the light switch and said, "I've wanted you since the day we met. Let's do this."

With the curtains of the bedroom window pushed back, moonlight shined on the bed's center. Our very own stage blessed with a diamond glow. Couldn't ask for better mood lighting.

Daryl pulled my blouse over my head. I unstrapped my bra, then slid back against the bed, pushing my shorts and panties off my feet. Exposed—naked and free—with a Daryl-only invitation.

He slithered between me. The one-eyed one-foot bandit thumped its hard head against my torso. I twitched.

I was in the zone.

Daryl's hot breath blew over my breasts while his main cane sandwiched between our bellies. Damn, heartbeats skipped to sprinter speed. Nipples so hard and beak-like pointy I thought they would slice Daryl's chest.

Flesh against flesh. His body heat merging with mine. Lawd.

I stroked the back of Daryl's head. Our lips found each other, dancing to a groove serenaded by fire and desire. Yes. About damn time.

Let the Olymp-dick games begin.

Chapter 19

"Damn, I've wanted you," I whispered.

Daryl mapped his lips down my cheek ... then my neck ... lawd ... until his tongue found my nipples. Sucked and slurped on 'em like raspberry-flavored Popsicles. Hittin' all the spots, dang. Nerve endings inside me all outta wack; a gazillion tingles buzzed in and around my butt bone. My toes curled until the joints popped.

I spread my legs wider, swiping my tongue across his lips. Two fingers skinny-dipped in and out of me. I twitched again. And again. Electric jolts ... ramming me hard. Damn. I was so *wet!* Like a swamp down there, you hear me? Daryl had that kinda power, long before he even dropped his pants.

"F-Fuck," I whispered. And "f-fuck" was an understatement. I cursed in whispers so much you woulda thought I was rapping a new version of the "Whisper Song." Moans mixed with heavy breaths and created high-pitched wails I hadn't heard from Michelle in a while.

Within seconds, Daryl's suckle-slurp finger-stroke combo shot razor-sharp pricks through me, from my head to my damn toes. Then they meshed and mushroomed into one big beehive, scorching the skin around my watery triangle, stabbing my inner thighs. Damn. So fast! Never saw it "comin'." Hit me so hard and quick I thought my toenails would crack.

"Shheeiiit!" I cried, my toes trying to dig into the mattress. Fuck the whispers. Time to let out the howls.

I raised Daryl's chin with my index finger, peeling his lips away from my swollen nipples. Jabbed my tongue in his mouth to muffle the cries-moans-cuss words erupting from the pit of my gut.

You know that didn't work. The thunder rolls inside my body roared and fuck—I couldn't hold back. I ripped my mouth from Daryl, crying out so loud I swear the folks up on San Jacinto Mountain heard me.

Damn, so easy. I'd been away from the feel of a man for far too long.

And I hadn't even tested the King Dingaling ... *yet*.

It thumped my chest for the umpteenth time. After catching my breath, I whispered, "I want it inside me. *Now*."

Hmmph. I *thought* I was ready for it, but for some reason, one important fact failed to register: That fool was going to stick a twelve-and-a-half inch rod between my legs!

Daryl raised up, grabbing the head of his bat for entry—but panic kicked in. I wanted to say, "hold on," but at that moment, he wedged King Dingaling inside my over-lubricated tunnel.

Girl, after that, anything that left these lips didn't make a lick of sense.

"Hold on" became a garbled "Hoodiehoo," like I was chanting some old rap lyric by Master P. English was no longer my primary language. The mighty python slithered deeper inside—not too deep—but enough to postpone motor skills for a hot second. I swear I went into shock.

And he was only a little over halfway in.

But remember this: I ain't had none in damn-near five months and here I go breaking my dry spell with a man hung like an elephant. What a way to jump back into the game, huh?

He began with slow, short strokes. "*Damn*," he whispered, "*you feel good as hell.*"

I wanted to say the same thing, but the more he stroked, the less my tongue worked.

I wrapped my hands around his biceps, clenching my teeth. Squeezed my eyeballs tighter as the pace and length of his strokes hit different speeds, scrubbing against my wet walls, scratching the surface of superhuman pleasure. In. Out. Back. Forth. Side-to-side.

"Shhhiatch!" I cried. "Fuagleit!"

Don't ask me what the fuck I was saying. I don't know. Speaking in tongues.

I bit my bottom lip and tore the skin, but ignored the pain. Sweat trickled down my forehead. Got hot quick up in there. I curled my toes so hard I thought I would snap a bone.

Lawd. Dick refreshment. Just what the doctor ordered.

He kept it comin'. Damn, a thesaurus couldn't detail the animalistic bliss ravaging my body. Ol' boy hit spots even *I* couldn't touch with my trusty toy at home. I probably sounded like a fool talking underwater.

He switched it up on me, worked circles, side-to-side, up, down, in and out. Strummed my clit like a damn banjo, too. And yes, I grooved with him. We rocked steady.

And King Dingaling *still* kept it comin', never allowing me to recover. My fingers clawed into Daryl's back. And scratched. Then raked. Daryl grunted, but somehow held it together. My hands then slipped off his back and fell to the bed. I tried to crush the sheets inside my fists, then started reaching for shit that wasn't even there.

Damn, it felt good, girl, you just don't know! I wanted to cry and laugh at the same time. And I did, actually, giggling for no reason while tears slid from the corners of my eyes. Oh-so happy tears.

I really had to be careful, though.

To prevent injury, Daryl raised his torso high so not to jab his Boa Constrictdick all the way in. More concerned with my "safety" than his own pleasure. What a sweetheart.

That shit did not matter, though. He still had me flopping around on that bed, kicking like a fish out of water. I rubbed all over his head and screamed at the top of my lungs. Didn't give a damn about who could hear me. Fuck 'em. Fuck 'em all. I was gettin' worked up in here and I *loooooooved* it. Um-um good.

It's funny. Curse words tumbled out my mouth like I had a case of profanity tourettes. Then the letters twisted around. Started screaming cartoon stuff like, "Shamn! Fit! Duck!" Shoot, I even made up *new* words. In between my garbled screams, I swear I squealed:

"You are so ... *f-f-f-f-fuckalicious!*"

Yes, I did, girl. Yes, I did.

As I was wilding out, my two babies flopped around like water balloons. Shoot, I felt like I'd burst all my body's sweat glands. Salty moisture covered my face, slipping into my eyes and mouth, mixing with tears. Damn. My body ain't never produced that much sweat, even when we strolled in ninety-degree desert heat. But I wasn't satisfied. Time to turn it up a notch.

I got bold with mine. I managed to whisper *"deeper."* He obliged.

Oh, *boy*.

Talk about the next frontier. Daryl dipped in at least an extra four inches. My eyeballs damn near blew up.

"Wooooo!" I screamed.

And then the rumbles came again. And again. And a-fuckin'-gain.

Four times. In fifteen minutes. Yes, I know. I should be on *Ripley's Believe it or Not*.

And I *still* wasn't done. Why stop when King Dingaling was hitting my G, H *and* I-spots? Had me sounding like an opera singer who could crack glass up in there!

But then I felt the urge.

I don't know what came over me, but I was on some "I am woman!" shit. Started feeling like an Amazon warrior princess. Invincible. I made Daryl stop so we could switch.

My turn.

He eased Dynamic Ding Dong out of me. We rolled around a bit until *I* was on top. Time to take the controls.

"Woooo!" I said again, wiping my forehead with the back of my hand. Daryl took the sheet and swiped it across his face. I glared at him, arching my lips into an I'm-'bout-to-tear-this-shit-up grin.

"I'm not through with yo' ass, yet," I said to King Dingaling, struggling for air.

I rested my sweaty palms on Daryl's beefcake chest. He said, "Chelle, be careful, now."

I didn't respond, just smiled, setting my sights on his rock cock. Felt like I had something to prove! I was ready to get prehistoric on his ass!

Super-duper ding-dong lay against Daryl's chest like a steel pipe, the condom still snug. Then idiot mode kicked in.

Without any kind of thought process warning of the obvious, I grabbed that piece of steel and held that bitch at attention. I raised up—then pushed down on him. *Hard.*

And I mean, *all the way down on him.* Girl! Girl! *Girl!*

Believe it or not, I swallowed his hard hot link *whole.* Dang, I didn't know ol' coochie had skills like that.

But for the rest of me, I couldn't move. Shoot, how could I move anything? A freakin' missile stabbed my insides, damn near shredding the walls of my vagina and puncturing my cervix. Intense pain split through me. My mouth hung open, but nothing came out except stunted snorts. Lawd ... the *pain.* I swear the head of his rocket stuck in the back of my throat. I couldn't see myself, but I'm sure it had me cross-eyed. Geez.

I imagine a man feeling the same way when kicked in the balls with steel toe boots.

Daryl set both hands on my hips and gently raised me off him. I fell back on the mattress and balled myself into a fetal position, trying to yank in air through clenched teeth.

What the hell was I thinking?

In the midst of enduring discomfort that had reached medieval torture level, I parted my lips and slid a thumb in my mouth. Why, I don't know. Didn't take long for me to realize I was ... sucking my thumb.

Wait a minute, I thought. *Am I sucking my thumb? Why am I sucking my thumb? I don't ... I'll be damned.*

Can you believe it? I was *sucking my thumb!* The last time I sucked my thumb Will Smith was still The Fresh Prince—*before* the show.

With my eyelids sealed tight, I somehow kept myself from wailing. I didn't know what to say to Daryl, so I lay alongside the edge of the bed with my back to him. He got up and flicked on the light. When I lifted my eyelids, I found Daryl kneeling in front of me, his gorgeous Arabesque face just inches from mine.

He stroked my arm. "Baby, why did you do that?" I heard genuine concern in his voice.

It took me a moment to respond, but when I tried to say something, I realized I was trembling.

I pulled my thumb out of my mouth. "I ... I ... d-don't know."

He sighed and shook his head. "*This always happens*," he whispered. Then he said, "Need me to get some ice?"

I didn't think ice would help, unless he had a foot-long popsicle in the freezer. I shook my head.

"Baby," he said, "you are drenched. I'm gonna get some water and a towel to wipe you off, okay?"

I nodded, then closed my eyes.

Soon after he left the room I heard the toilet flush; I assume to get rid of the condom. Made me feel a little guilty, ya know? I don't think my baby had the pleasure of five big O's like I did.

Damn, that's a thought, though...

Couldn't imagine his rifle shooting a million sperm pellets up inside me. With all that power? Shoot, his load probably would've fired through the rubber and blew my head off.

Minutes later, Daryl returned with a damp towel and tall glass of ice water. I wanted to stay in my balled-up position, but a sista's dry throat said "forget that." He knelt down next to the bed. I raised myself up and rested on my elbow.

"Thank you," I said, my voice all groggy. Knocked the glass back and didn't stop until it was empty.

"Damn, you *were* thirsty," he said.

I placed the empty glass on the nightstand. Didn't want to face him—too embarrassed, I guess. I managed a smile, but was afraid to move too much.

Daryl turned off the light and slid in behind me. The soft feel of the towel soon caressed my arms, back, and neck. After he wiped me down, he massaged my shoulders with his large hands. It felt pretty damn good, enough to forget about some of the pain.

"I'm sorry," I said. "I wish I hadn't done that."

"No, baby, *I'm* sorry," Daryl replied. "I should've told you a long time ago, but I didn't want to scare you off. As I said, I had problems in the past." He sighed. "We just have to work around this. How 'bout I cut it in half? Six inches should be cool, right?"

I tried to chuckle, but managed a few "uhs" and "ows" instead.

"We definitely don't want to do that, baby," I said. "I just have to be more careful next time."

He started to talk again, but I tuned him out because my jumbled thoughts took me to another channel:

Damn, I've never been screwed so good in my life! We didn't go on for more than thirty minutes, but it felt like thirty hours. Boy, it was off da hook, but now I'm laying here sore as hell and crunched over while this beautiful man strokes my back. Never thought riding a man could be ... fatal. I know Daryl can't help being that big, but ... can I handle this?

Chapter 20

I pried my eyes open, turned to the clock, and saw the numbers 7-3-4. In my morning haze, I noticed a glass of water next to the lamp. A welcome sight, let me tell you. I reached for the glass.

"Ow," I said, wincing. Damn, reaching for a glass of freakin' water ignited an ache in my shoulder I didn't know I had.

In what seemed like one gulp, I drained the glass of water. When I tried to sit up, a sharp pain pierced my lower back, though that was nothing compared to the fire down below. Like someone had taken a chainsaw to my cooch.

"Ugh!" I grunted.

What the hell? I had woken up to a new band of body distress. Even though sore spots twisted my face, I managed a smile when I remembered why I hurt so good: Daryl.

Expecting to see my baby lying next to me, I rolled to my other side, slower than an old man in a body cast. I frowned. No Daryl.

Where the hell is he now? I thought. My inner temperature rose. *Can I wake up next to my man, damn!*

The sound of a toilet flushing cut into my thoughts. I then heard the sink and seconds later, Daryl opened the door. He wore a robe and held another one under his arm. He smiled when he noticed me awake.

"Good morning," he said. "You feeling aw'ight?"

I pulled the sheets up to my neck. "I'm okay," I replied, lying. "A little sore, though."

He sat by my feet and handed me the robe. "You sure?"

"Yea—ow!" I cried, trying once again to sit up. "Okay, a *lot* sore. I'll be all right, though."

He looked away. We sat quiet for a moment, both of us nodding. Kind of uncomfortable, actually, not knowing what to say. Our primal bump-and-hump episode didn't exactly have a happy ending. I know I was definitely embarrassed. Damn, I acted the fool the night before. King Dingaling had woken the she-devil in me. Lawd.

I broke our silence. "So, um, what do you want to do today?"

"Don't know. Thought maybe we could shop a little. We have to check out by noon. You hungry?"

I rotated my neck. "Yes. We still got those chimichangas in the fridge."

"Naw, you don't want to eat that. Probably no good, anyway. Let's have a nice breakfast."

I smiled. "Okay." I pushed my arm through the robe. "Will you help me up? Need to potty."

He stood and grabbed my hand. "Sure, babe."

As I rose out of bed, my two babies flashed him. I chuckled, then covered up.

"Thank you," I said, turning my face from him. Wasn't trying to be rude, but I'm sure my morning breath smelled like purified funk.

I slid my feet across the carpet instead of taking footsteps like a normal human being, inching my way toward the bathroom. Sheesh. A ninety-year-old woman with a stroller could walk faster.

Got in the bathroom, sat on the toilet, and tried to let it all out. Oh, lawd. I thought I would crack a tooth, clamping down so hard. The stream gushed against what felt like a million tears within my comatose coochie.

"You all right in there?" Daryl asked, tapping the door.

That's when I realized I was grunting. "I ... *wooo* ... I'm all right. I'll be out in a m-minute."

"Don't rush. I'm gonna take a shower in the office."

"Yow ... okay."

My feet slapped the tiles. "*Wooo*," I whispered, "*Is it gonna be like this all the time? I don't know if I can do this again!*"

After our showers, we dressed for our last day in Palm Springs. Streams of hot, steamy water had helped relieve some aches, but I couldn't do a damn thing about my injured sugar walls.

Daryl reached under his shirt and rubbed his back. He hissed a few times and I looked up, noticing his face all twisted.

"You okay?" I asked. "Need me to scratch your back?"

"No, I think you did a good job of that last night. Ow!"

I rolled my eyes. "Ha, ha. Funny. I know I got a little rowdy. I'm sorry. Does it hurt that bad?"

"It's cool," he said, shrugging. "Hurts a little bit, but I'll be aw'ight."

"Let me see."

He waved me off. "Chelle, I'm cool. Don't worry—"

"Please?"

He stared at me for a moment, twisting his lips around. "Okay."

Turning his back to me, Daryl pulled up his shirt. I expected a few scratches here and there. Nothing crazy.

Yeah, right. I had to cover my mouth to muffle the gasps.

"What?" Daryl said. "How bad is it?"

Dayum! I did that? It took me a moment to respond. "Um ... I ... scratched you up pretty good."

What an understatement. I had no idea I did so much damage. Like the marks of Zorro on each side of his spine. I had turned his flesh into mincemeat, pretty much marking my territory.

When I ran my fingers against his skin, he twitched. "Ow. Careful."

"I need to put something on your back. This is pretty raw."

"I have some antibiotic cream in one of my bags. Hold on."

Daryl walked over to his tote bag and pulled out a small first aid kit. He handed me the Neosporin.

I rubbed it along each of the scratches. Dang, I really Freddy Kruegered his whole back.

"Damn," I said, flashing back to last night, "I bet I made a lot of noise, huh?" I chuckled. "You think all that screaming and cursing had something to do with someone's secret weapon?"

"Don't know," Daryl said, giggling. "Maybe."

"Maybe? Whatever." I rubbed his lower back. "Shoot. I wonder if anybody heard me?"

He shook his head. "Naw. I'm sure it was cool. Walls are pretty thick."

Yeah, right.

As I stepped out of the room, a boy and girl almost knocked me over, tearing down the hallway. They were about eight or nine, wearing cute little swim gear and towels draped over their shoulders, their stringy blond hair drenched and stuck to their foreheads.

My first thought was, *where are their parents to whip their asses? Running up and down the hallways like they lost their minds!*

They stopped at the door next to ours. When the boy saw me, his eyes widened; then he whispered something in the girl's ear.

The little girl stroked her ponytail. "Good morning."

Daryl and I replied, "Good morning."

We didn't move four feet before the little heifer stopped us dead in our tracks. She looked at me and said, "What was all that screaming about? We heard it from your room."

I said, "Excuse me?"

The little boy scratched his head. "All that screaming woke us up last night. Was that you? Were you in pain?"

"Um ... well, that's—"

None of your damn business! I wanted to say.

Daryl cupped his hand over his lips, about to bust up laughing. I wanted to kick him.

"Yeah, I was ... uh ... in pain. Bad stomach ache." That statement held some truth.

"Stomach aches can do that?"

I nodded. "Yup."

The boy scratched the side of his nose. With his head tilted, he shot me an odd look. "You were pretty loud," he said. "Sounded like a donkey."

Daryl collapsed against the wall, just rolling. I couldn't help but chuckle a little, too. I probably *did* sound like a wild animal.

I reached back and slapped Daryl's stomach. "Yeah, um, well, you kids have a nice day."

"You, too," the little girl said, waving. "If you need Rolaids or something, my mom has some. You want me to ask her? She's in the room right—"

"Don't worry about it, kid. Thanks, anyway."

I hobbled past them, ignoring the spasms ripping between my thighs. Just wanted to escape the heat of humiliation.

I turned to Daryl. He threw his hand over his mouth again.

"Shut up!" I cried, although he hadn't said anything. "Nobody heard us, huh? Okay. It's your fault they heard me, any damn way. Punk."

I thought Daryl would fall out from laughing so hard. I just kept it moving, as much as I could.

We had a nice breakfast, but the wooden chair didn't help a sista's tender coochie. I moved my legs all around, trying to find the best position. Got to a point where I said, "oh well" and sat with my legs spread like a man.

After breakfast, we went downtown and hit a few shops. My "pimp limp" mimicked Daryl's strut, so I didn't feel that bad about walking like I had a pencil stuck up my butt. I did get tired of people asking me, "are you all right?" I played it off, said I'd pulled my groin muscle. Once again, it was almost true.

Got back to the hotel room about an hour later and packed our stuff. While Daryl did an OCD sweep of the office and living room, the bed seized my attention.

The bedsheets and blankets were as we'd left them—ruffled, wrinkled and saturated with remnants of last night. I stared at the spot where Daryl and I had done the damn thang. Woooo, lawd. Leaning against the dresser, I took in a deep breath.

Daryl had revealed his King Dingaling alter ego the night before, and went from Clark Kent to Superman, warping my mind with strokes that caused earthquakes within me. Rocked my world so hard my screams sent shock waves throughout the whole freakin' hotel.

Until that night, I didn't know a man's penis could make your teeth click, eyes cross, knees knock, skin peel back, geez. And I never experienced that many orgasms in one night before. No man had *ever* done that to me, even my ex. *Ever.* Wow. Crazy. The mix of my dry spell, alcohol, Daryl, and his bionic weapon created the perfect platform for insane body tremors. And a sore coochie.

Damn. What a night.

The corners of my lips inched up. I reached into my purse and yanked out the digital camera. Took two snaps of the bed—my own secret Kodak moments. I wanted to remember the spot where I had first become one with Daryl forever.

A sound from the living room jolted me out of my sweet memory. I rushed the camera inside my purse. Daryl walked in a second later.

"Hey, did I see a flash?" he asked.

I shook my head. "Nope. Not in here."

His eyelids lowered. "Not in here, huh?"

I knew my conscience would get the best of me, so I said, "All right, all right. I took a couple of pictures."

He frowned. "Of what?"

"The bed."

Daryl laughed. "The bed? Why?"

I shrugged. "Well, you know ... first time we did it. Special moment for me."

Daryl took my hand, pulled me close and wet my lips with a long kiss. "Me too, babe."

I smiled, burying my head against his chest. Nothing else mattered at that moment. "Okay, babe," he said, releasing a long breath. "It's almost noon. We need to roll. Ready?"

I looked around the room one last time. "Yeah, I'm ready. Back to reality."

Sore coochie and all.

Chapter 21

Buh-bye Palm Springs. Thanks for the memories. Dang, Daryl dropped the bomb harder than the Gap Band on a sista. Blew my mind! Still can't believe how big that thing is. How in the world does he walk around—

"Hey," Daryl said, turning down the radio. "How ya doin' over there?"

I took in a breath. "I'm fine."

With my seat leaned back, I almost touched the backseat. I spread my legs in a V angle for a little relief.

Daryl said, "Did you have a good time?"

"Sure did. Wish we could've stayed a little longer."

He nodded, but didn't say a word. Silence again, except for Rihanna screaming in her crackly voice.

The questions in my head picked at me, so out of nowhere, I said, "Daryl, how in the world do you keep that thing from getting hard and slapping against your forehead as you go about your business? Shoot, it's long enough."

He rolled when I said that. "Chelle, you are a trip! That's why I love being with you. Always crackin' a brotha up." He looked at me and winked.

I cracked a grin. "Yeah, I'm a riot."

"Yes, you are." He paused for a second while tapping the wheel, then said, "Well, it's basically mind over matter."

I tilted my head. "What do you mean?"

"In the seventh grade I had this old, scraggly, wrinkled up Social Studies teacher named Mrs. Thigpen. We called her Mrs. Pigpen because she was nasty as hell."

I chuckled.

He said, "She was always digging up her nose, flicking boogers while we took tests."

"Ugh! Stop!"

"I'm serious! At that age, I was pretty big down there, so to keep from having an 'accident' around girls, I'd think of her. Getting hard is the last thing that happens when you think of something like that! Well ... until I met you."

I smiled. "Me? Oh, hush."

He shook his head. "That first night we almost did the do in my apartment, Mrs. Thigpen wasn't working. And I thought I had that shit to a science. That's when I realized I felt something deeper for you. More than just a one night stand, I guess."

Wow. A thousand tingles sprinkled through me. For a second, I couldn't say anything, just let his words sink in. I'd never met a man who was willing to deny himself sexual relief because he wanted to do things "right," especially with the other "head" trying to call the shots. He could've hit it the first night—believe me, I was game—but he refused. The man was sumn' else.

"That's so sweet, Daryl," I said. "I always wondered why you backed off. Now I know."

He cut into the left lane and sped past a minivan with a Brady Bunch inside. "Yes, you do. Ever since I was young, I've had to come up with new ways to hide my gift. Long shirts, baggy or loose pants, shorts that stretch over my knees—whatever worked. If I sit a certain way without trying to hide it, it can be pretty easy to notice the ... uh ... bulge."

A picture of Daryl popped in my head—him sitting in a chair, legs spread like wings, a bulge the size of a football pressing his pants. The point was clear.

I said, "Wow. You're right. I'm actually surprised I still didn't notice."

"Yup. All about shifting your focus away from the area. I have to move my leg a certain way, cover it up with a briefcase, bag—anything. I've learned to be pretty creative."

"Shoot, you fooled me."

I almost slipped and mentioned seeing him in slacks when I was stalking him that day. I caught myself and said, "What about when you have to wear slacks and your shirt tucked in?"

"Well," he said, "I have to wear pleated slacks. Gives me good room down there. Believe it or not, I sometimes tape it to my leg, too. When we went to the movies, I had tape on it then, for example."

I raised my head. "Whaaaaaaat?"

"No joke."

"Damn, that's weird! What, duct tape?"

He laughed. "What? No! The kind of tape they use for bandages."

I shook my head. "Wow. Hmmm ... you ever hurt it?"

"Shoot, all the time. Remember how uncomfortable I was on that horse?"

"Yes."

"Well, picture a know-it-all seventeen-year-old bouncing up and down on his uncle's horse going almost full speed when his woody gets crushed between his butt and the saddle."

I balled my fist and clenched my whole body. "Ow! Probably worse than what I feel like now."

"Maybe. My shit was all bent up," Daryl said. "Worst pain of my life."

"Geez. So were you all right after I made you ride that horse?"

"Yup, I managed. Just had a few painful flashbacks."

I touched his leg. "I'm so sorry, baby."

"It's all good," he said. "Funny thing is guys talk about having a big yang and women dream about finding a man with one. But having to lug one around all day is a different story, for real. I basically have a third leg, you know what I mean?"

"Yeah," I said, giggling.

I gazed at the desert hills outside Daryl's window. Flashed back to when me and Charlotte were screaming and laughing about finding a man with a superhero penis. Crazy how I wound up with one shortly after. Man. What are the odds? Charlotte wouldn't believe my luck.

Never thought about the burden it places on a man, though. Shoot, it wasn't exactly a walk in the park for the female either, as my broken poontang could attest. "Wow," I said, my thoughts all over the mental map. "I guess it's the same for women with huge breasts. Men go on and on about how they love big titties, but a lot of those women can't wait to get rid of them because of the back pain."

"Yup. No doubt. Believe it or not, I had major problems trying to lose my virginity back in the day."

"Get outta here."

He shook his head. "No lie. When I was about fourteen, my virgin girlfriend took one look at my thing and almost peed her pants. I've actually gotten that reaction a lot, which is why I'm cautious about 'whipping it out' when I meet someone new. I had an ex who couldn't take the pain, so she dipped out on a brotha."

"Damn," I said, not surprised. My mind went away again. "I truly never thought of it that way."

I imagined myself as a fourteen-year-old girl, heart pounding, face sweating, fingers twitching—eager to see a boy's ding-a-ling, only to find a ding-a-*long*. Shoot, I can't blame that girl. If some boy whipped out a log to poke between my legs, I probably would've passed out, too. A penis the size of a small tree can do that to you.

"Yup, me and my boy are one of a kind."

"You can say that again." I fanned myself. "So do you have a name for 'your boy'?" I didn't mention anything about the dozen or so names I'd given it.

Daryl threw his head against his seat, screaming with laughter. "Aw man!" he cried, sounding like someone choking. "Back in the day, I had crazy names! Cock Diesel, Penis Genius, Meter of Peter ... uh ... Dick Tracy!"

"Dick Tracy?" I laughed so hard my knees curled up, despite the pain between my legs. I guess when you have something as absurd as a foot-long penis, it deserves a name like "Cock Diesel" or "Dick Tracy."

"Yeah," he said, wiping his eyes. "It's been more of a curse than a blessing, though. I was so self-conscious I didn't go to my prom; couldn't wear the fly tight jeans; didn't wear shorts a lot, even when it was blazin' hot outside. No different today, except I'm not as self-conscious anymore." He snickered. "Well, maybe just a little. I hate standing in front of a group, giving a presentation or something. I always feel like people are staring at it."

My smiles faded. Daryl gave me a whole new point of view; almost sounded like he had a handicap. Such a load to carry—literally.

"Don't get me wrong," he said, cutting into my thoughts, "you don't have to feel sorry for a brotha. Me and my boy could have far worse problems, right?"

I nodded. "Yeah, I guess you're right. Definitely won't be givin' you, uh, 'oral attention,' though. You might mess around and realign my jaw or something."

Laughter erupted from him. I laughed, too, but I really wasn't looking for chuckles. Had other shit on my mind. Crap that bugged me.

I wondered if I could have a normal sex life with that thing. "Normal" really wasn't the word 'cause I figured I would have to suffer endless days of sore coochieitis. And what if Daryl and I broke up? My punani would be an endless tunnel that an average-sized man would get lost in.

Daryl is a special guy, but ... is it worth it?

Chapter 22

We got back to our complex a little after four in the afternoon. As I reached for the door handle, Daryl grabbed my elbow.

"Wait," he said.

Daryl opened his door and stepped out. I shook my head and smiled as he walked around to my side.

He grabbed the handle and pulled my door. "Here ya go."

I donned my shades before I slid my leg out. He took my hand, holding a watchful eye. I placed both feet on the pavement. "Boy, you are too good to me."

"Is there any other way I should be?"

I didn't know how to respond except to shake my head with a smile. Damn. So many smiles since Daryl "U-hauled" into my life.

I grabbed my shopping bags out of the backseat while he took care of our luggage. He strapped two bags over one shoulder, one over the other, and held my tote bag in his hand. With all that weight hanging off his limbs, he still managed to close the hatch.

"Damn," I said, impressed. "You got all that?"

"Yeah, I'm cool," he replied, jiggling the keys in his hand. He even took the shopping bags from me. "I'll bring your bags up after I drop mine off since we're closer to my apartment. Do you need help up the stairs?"

"No, no," I said, stepping away. "I can make it."

"You sure?"

I stepped onto the sidewalk. "I'm fine. I got my new pimp walk down now."

We laughed, kissed and parted ways.

I stepped up the steps to my apartment, my pace no faster than a crawl. My tender spots didn't hurt as much, but still enough to make me wince when I moved.

After fumbling with my keys, I nudged the door. "Home sweet home."

I slid my shoes off and beelined toward the potty. Still had to handle my business in squirts; no steady streams for at least two more days.

To heal my ill "na-na" and all the other body parts that ached, I decided to soak in a hot bath. While I waited for the tub to fill up, I lit some incense. Couldn't wait to submerge myself in soapy bubbles. Definitely what the doctor ordered.

I had just shed all my clothes when I heard a knock. Wrapping myself in a robe, I went to the front door. "Hey, you."

Daryl walked in with my luggage. "Hey, sexy. Damn, you all dressed up in a robe already?"

"Yeah. 'Bout to take a bath."

"Nice." He took in a big whiff. "Mmm, smells good up in here. You love you some incense, huh?"

I closed the door. "Yup."

"I need to remember that," he said, smiling. "So, you want me to put these in your bedroom?"

"Yes, please."

He dropped the bags next to my bed and set his hands on his hips. His gaze roamed the room.

"Why are you looking around?" I asked.

"Damn," he said. "I just realized something."

"What?"

"I've never been in your bedroom before."

I put my finger to my lips. "Hmmm. I wonder why?"

"Oh, you got jokes, huh?" He eased his arms around my waist. "Well, we might just have to change that, huh?"

His lips felt nice and warm. "That sounds like a great idea. Only took you like six-and-a-half weeks to figure it out!"

"Yeah, whatever." We savored each other once more. "Well, enjoy your bath. I'm going back to the crib to take care of some stuff. I'll call you a little later to check up on you, aw'ight?"

He was so thoughtful. And real. Another smile graced my lips. "Sounds like a plan."

I followed him to the front door. "By the way," Daryl said, his hand on the doorknob, "I do, too."

I cocked my head sideways. "You do what?"

He turned to me, his lips curved upward. His eyes yearned for me, like they were saying my name.

"I do ... love you."

My bottom lip fainted. I couldn't speak.

Damn. His words caressed my ears, trickled down to my feet and seeped out my eyes in the form of warm tears. Even with parted lips, I still could not muster any words.

He cut a stream of moisture with his thumb. "Are you all right?"

Through lips that quivered, I said, "I thought you were asleep. You ... heard me?"

He nodded.

A tear smacked the carpet. I buried my head in his chest. "I'm so embarrassed."

"Don't be." His chin tapped my forehead. "Like I said, the feeling is very mutual."

We kissed. My heart swelled for this man. My king. If Ms. Coochie wasn't still out of commission, I would have taken him back to my bedroom to show him how much he meant to me.

Maybe things will feel better after my bath. Naw, probably not.

Awwww. Just what I needed.

Like heaven on earth to soak my body in water damn near the boiling point under mountains of bubbles. Four lit candles waft a ginger peach aroma. Steam has fogged up my cabinet mirror so much it looks like somebody painted it silver.

That's where I am now, soothing my sore spots with a therapy bath, my head against a bath pillow, trying to forget the pain from a twelve-in-a-half inch thrashing. Damn. It's not Daryl's fault for having an elephant trunk between his legs. I was the dumb ass, jumping on that thing like a bull in a rodeo.

And now here I lay ... alone ... staring at the ceiling, thinking about Daryl and King Dingaling. Mr. Pleasure-before-Pain. A *lot* of pain.

Damn, the Bionic Dick rattled my bones, girl. I didn't want the bump-and-grind to ever stop. What woman would? Whatever it could give, that's what I wanted to take. Until the hotel security, Palm Springs law enforcement—even the FBI came knocking.

But 'cha know what? That way of thinking made my happy ass lay up in a fetal position on the edge of a hotel bed.

Shit. What to do?

And Daryl ... damn.

I can't say enough about that man. Never met anyone so sweet, so giving, so ... whatever else. Hmmm. And I'm sure a lot of women wouldn't mind taking a long trip on a Mandingo.

But that brings me back to my original point, this whole can-I-make-this-relationship-work thing.

What woman wouldn't want a man with a foot long stick dick? Shoot, I thought I did. Now, I'm not so sure. I now know first-hand what it feels like and let me tell you, there's too much potential for irreparable damage. I could wind up in the hospital with a twisted spine and vagina walls lookin' like soggy shredded wheat, shit.

And you know what? I've been so wrapped in this natural Daryl-induced high, the cloud around my head keeps me from seeing the light. Maybe things aren't so "peachy" between us. Or at least, they won't stay that way.

Is Daryl really that perfect? What man is?

Well ... he did say he loves me, though. Such the sweetest thing. But...

I don't know. I bet I haven't seen the true Daryl, yet. I mean, really, he's probably an asshole, like a lot of men, just frontin'. Hmmph, wouldn't doubt it. Men tend to change once they realize they "got you." Pull a 360 on your ass.

Maybe we should just break up now? He's bound to pull the rug from under my feet eventually, right? I'm tired of men with issues, too. Baggage. If it took that long to tell me about his "gift," would Daryl later become comfortable holding back more truth from me as our relationship grew? Start telling lies, maybe? Even cheating? I couldn't stand it. Screw that shit. Only one thing can help me avoid potential floods of dishonesty.

No way around it. I think I need to kick his ass to the curb.

To hell with that. I wasn't finished yet.

I wore my robe, half-stepping with a vengeance to Daryl's apartment. My booty peek-a-booed as the tail of my robe swung with every hard step. No shoes, no clothes—I didn't give a damn. Three o'clock in the morning under a dark sky and diamond moon, work in less than five hours—still didn't give a damn.

I wanted a rematch.

The steps felt coarse under my feet. Took two seconds to get to the top. "That punk better be home."

I pounded on the door. Waited. My feet tapped the cement, hands on my hips. Pounded three more times. Waited.

The door crept open, its hinges squeaking. He stood in the dark living room, shirtless. The moonlight made his brown skin sparkle and he held the grin of a demon, his fiery eyes matching the fury in my own.

"I knew you'd come back," he said. "Let's do this."

My sentiments exactly. "Let's do this."

Yeah, I was ready for it, and "it" got ready for me.

Curved and hard, long and stretching longer, King Dingaling protruded in my direction like Pinocchio's nose after a dozen lies. That didn't phase me, though. Uh-uh, I ain't skurred, even though it grew to 13 ... 14 ... 15 ... eventually, 18 inches. That's right, *18*. I told Daryl the Jedi Knight Meat Master and his foot-in-a-half light saber to come with it!

My robe fell to the floor. He bent me over the armrest of the couch and spread my legs, hands gripping the cushion, my booty up high and firm.

"Come on, Meat Master!" I screamed. "Give it to me! Give it to me. Give it to—ugh!"

He snaked inside me, but stopped halfway. He started slow, stepped up his speed, then pounded me in a fast and furious rhythm. Rock-hard momentum made my braids sway, titties smacking the sides of my cheeks. My nails sliced holes in the couch cushion.

But forget that small stuff. I wanted all 18 inches.

"Deeper!" I screamed. "Deeper! Give me all of it!"

His fingers clutched my butt cheeks tighter. "I don't think you want that."

I slammed my fist. "Don't tell me what I want!" I cried. "I want it—aw!"

Why the hell did I say that?

I felt my walls tearing. Hard flesh inflated inside me. Once again, I underestimated what I was getting into. Shoot, what was getting into *me*.

"No!" I cried. "Stop it! I didn't mean it! I—"

"You said you wanted deeper." His voice was calm ... eerily calm. "So that's what you're gonna get. You ready for the last nine inches?"

I kicked with all my strength, my toes digging into the carpet, knees banging against the couch. Screamed as loud as I could, stabbing my nails into the cushions to pull myself away from him.

"No!" I cried. "Stop it!"

He gripped me tighter. "Okay! Here it comes!"

"No!" No one could hear my screams. "*Nooooooooo...*"

My screams jolted me awake. I sat straight up in bed, gasping for breath. Damn. Once again, Mr. Sandman revealed the answers I needed to know. I woke up sweating a pond and breathing so hard I thought my lungs would collapse.

"Wooo!" I cried, wiping my forehead. "What a nightmare! If that ain't a sign, I don't know what is! I know I'm kicking him to the curb now."

Chapter 23

One Year Later

Gas grill smoke dissolved in the fresh air of a late summer season. The smell of chicken still lingered, tickling the hairs in my nostrils and teasing my empty belly.

Damn, we need to eat soon, I thought.

I took a sip of iced tea and set the glass on the table. Then I heard giggling from inside the new gazebo.

"What 'chall doin' up in there?" I said.

"Nuttin'," Baby Boy cried back. "Me and Lorraine just checkin' out the inside."

I turned and saw the back of Lorraine's head through the screen window. Couldn't tell what she was doing, but it looked like she was leaning over the edge of the hot tub.

For some reason, that made the corners of my lips inch up. Just got the thing delivered a few days ago. In my dirty little mind, I could see me and my man under a million hot bubbles, sipping white wine and making "waves." Only spot on the new property we hadn't christened yet.

I shook away my Penthouse thoughts. "Hey! I said ya'll can look at it! Don't be trying to turn it on, now."

I heard a grunt. "Aw, c'mon now!" Baby Boy cried. "This is nice as hell! Never seen a TV and stereo system up in a gazebo before!" He poked his head out the entrance. "When you gonna hook it up?"

"Later tonight after you leave." I chuckled. "Ain't you supposed to be watching the grill, anyway? Check the chicken."

"Yeah, boy," Lorraine said, smacking her man's arm. "Get on over there."

Baby Boy shot me an evil look, but did what I told him. He turned off the grill, grabbed a long fork and plucked chicken into a large pan. Lorraine stood next to him, her hand on his shoulder.

I gazed at them for a moment. Such a cute couple. Lorraine's a "big-boned" sista with freckles, sporting thick locks that stopped at the shoulders. Baby Boy's been in the Navy less than a year and already calling her fiancée.

"Damn, where are they?" I said, looking at my watch. "They've been gone at least an hour."

"They should be back soon," Lorraine said. "You know they prolly goin' up and down the liquor aisles of every store 'round here."

I laughed. "I know that's right. Hey, you know what we need right now?"

Lorraine said, "What?"

"Some music!"

I jumped up, slid the patio door open and walked toward the living room. Grabbing Usher's new CD, I popped that bad boy into the CD player and cranked it up. Time to start this party off right!

When I walked back out, Baby Boy was snapping his fingers, talkin' 'bout, "What you know about that jam?"

I frowned. "Boy, shut up. I bought that CD."

I bobbed my head, sending a challenge to him through my eyes. My hips swayed to the rhythm.

I said, "Lorraine, Baby Boy's always talkin' smack 'bout how good he can dance. I want to see."

Baby Boy turned to Lorraine. Lorraine smiled, nodded, then moved closer to him. He rotated his NIKE hat to the back, then pimp-strolled toward me, trying to project a playalistic air of coolness. With Usher screaming in the background and the hard bass bumping the speakers, it didn't take long for us to partake in the backyard boogie.

We got our groove on, pretty much acting the fool and whatnot, doin' a miniature Soul Train line. Just having a damn good time.

Then I heard, "Charlotte's in the house!"

I turned and saw my girl standing by the patio door. She ran toward us. We all wrapped our arms around her.

My eyes lit up. "Where's the baby? Where's the baby?"

Just as I said that, Greg appeared, pushing baby Tia in a stroller. We rushed to him, leaving Charlotte standing by herself, hands on her hips.

"Now, how ya'll gonna just leave me like that?" she said.

Tia—my goddaughter, a beautiful brown angel—was wrapped up like a pure bundle of joy. The women formed a wall around the stroller and became rapt in this tiny human, our faces softening into affectionate beams of delight.

I heard Baby Boy say, "Damn. Look at these females."

"Yeah," Greg said, "they're always like this. Wait 'till you have one."

Baby Boy said, "Hell naw. Not any time soon." Lorraine slapped his arm.

I chuckled and kissed Greg on the cheek. "How ya doin', Greg?"

"Busy as hell." He wiped his brow with the back of his hand. "Ever since my agent sold the book, I've been trying to get a jumpstart on promotional stuff. You know, building a new web site, making fliers, postcards—everything." He shook his head. "On top of that, I got her and Charlotte to deal with."

Charlotte slapped her husband's arm. Smiling, he kissed her forehead.

"Yeah," she said, "don't be talkin' 'bout me, now. You're the reason she's here." We laughed.

Then Tammy and her boyfriend Terrell walked out with a cooler. Perfect timing. More fuel for the party.

Tammy embraced me and Lorraine, then "oooed" and "awwwed" toward Tia, making faces sillier than mine.

Terrell said, "We got Smirnoffs, San Miguels, Heineken, wine—you name it."

Baby Boy clapped his hands. "That's what I'm talkin' 'bout."

"Boy, you'd better get away from that cooler and get some grape juice," Tammy said, waving a finger at him.

We rolled. Damn, it felt good to be around good people. My friends. My family.

Only thing missing was my other half.

While everybody occupied themselves with the baby and each other, I wandered through the house. Saw big bowls of food on a dining room table waiting on us, but other than that, empty space.

I peeked outside. "Hey, Greg. Where is—"

"Right behind you."

Large hands slid under my elbows and around my arms. A hard chest pressed against my back. I blew a quiet sigh and smiled.

I said, "Why you gon' sneak up on me like that?"

He tickled his nose against my ear. "I wasn't gone that long, was I?"

I folded my arms. His warmth devoured me. "Long enough."

"I'm sorry." He turned to everyone. "Are we ready to eat?"

"Hell yeah!" Greg cried. "Hungry as hell!"

We all cosigned with Greg, so we got our grub on. While filling our tummies with barbecue chicken, pork chops, macaroni and cheese, greens and er' thing else, sunlight faded to dusk.

Afterwards, we sat around on lounge chairs and stools with full bellies, conversing and taking turns holding the baby. Soft jazz replaced Rap and R&B, in nice cadence with our chill mode. What a day. So many smiles, so much laughter. Felt good to be in an atmosphere where positive vibes flowed. This was my element. These were my peeps. .

And Daryl was my man. My King. My Everything.

Yeah, cheesy, but fuck it—it's true.

Daryl stood up. "Excuse me, baby. I need to do something real quick."

"What you fixin' to do?"

"Don't worry 'bout it," he said, grinning. "I'll be right back."

Daryl disappeared inside the house, and the music cut off shortly after.

Baby Boy cried, "Aw, man! C'mon! How you gon' stop Norman Brown? I was just gettin' into that!" We all joined him, griping and grunting.

Daryl reappeared, carrying a glass of champagne in each hand. I curled my brow. That familiar grin etched his face.

Uh-oh. He had something up his sleeve! Sneaky butt. I could see it in his eyes.

The night skies darkened our surroundings, so Greg flicked on the backyard lights.

"Excuse me," Daryl said, now standing beside me. "I need ya'll to listen up real quick."

Silence. All eyes on him.

"First off," he started, "I'd like to welcome and thank ya'll for coming to my new home. Sorry you San Diego folks had to drive sixty miles to get here, but a brotha wasn't even thinkin' 'bout plopping 400-thow down there for what I could get for 200 out here, you know? I love San Diego, but a brotha had to raise up."

We laughed. I ran my nails up and down the back of his leg.

"Anyway," he continued, "I'm glad you guys came out to my little housewarming shin dig. This means a lot to me."

"Well, after you begged us we didn't have a choice!" Charlotte said. The laughs kept coming.

"True, true. But this gathering isn't just about a new house." He turned to me. "It's about starting my new life with this woman right here."

My heartbeat double-timed. He handed me a glass and lifted my chin, capturing my eyes. "I love this woman to death, ya'll," he said, raising his glass. "Let's make a toast."

I noticed everyone had a glass of champagne in their hands. *What the...*

"To Michelle," Daryl said.

The rest of my peeps repeated his words. That shocked me 'cause they said my name in unison. Glasses tapped in my honor. I had no idea why, but I went with the flow. I lifted my glass to tap against Daryl's. That's when I saw it.

I screamed so loud my ears popped.

Laughter and handclaps erupted around me, but quickly died down when little Tia wailed her disapproval.

Lawd. Have. Mercy. My lips began to wobble; tears bubbled in the corner of my eyes the instant I realized what lay in the bottom of the glass.

He bent to one knee. I raised a shaky hand to my lips.

"Michelle Dana Larsen," he said. "Will you marry me?"

I set my wineglass down, then wiped my clammy hands on my shirt. Had to draw in all the air around me to calm my out-of-whack nerves. "Are you serious?"

"Does it look like I'm serious?" He took my hand. "Come on now, don't leave a brotha hanging in front of all these crazy people."

I screamed, "Boy, what do you think? Yes!"

I jumped up and wrapped my arms around his head so fast his face slammed into my shoulder.

"Don't give the man a concussion!" Terrell said.

Everyone laughed.

I lifted the glass to my mouth. The symbol of our union danced against my lips as champagne disappeared down my throat. I caught it with my teeth and locked down. That thing wasn't going nowhere. It was mine. *All* mine.

"Damn, don't eat it, now," Tammy said. "He has to put it on you." Daryl retrieved the ring from between my teeth and slipped it onto my finger. Such a perfect fit, glimmering as bright as the glow on my tear-stained face. I ran a finger over ten small diamonds surrounding a massive princess-cut rock. Damn! For lil' ol' me.

I tried, but couldn't restrain the hurricane of tears. Lawd.

I caught a flash out the corner of my eye. I turned my head to see Baby Boy snapping pics with his digital camera, a big ole grin on his face.

"There," Daryl said, smiling. "Looks beautiful on you."

My friends swarmed us. Everyone knew of this secret occasion, keeping it behind my back the whole time. Damn. I didn't think that was possible, especially with them having gossipy mouths like news anchors on CNN. They rained so many kisses and hugs on me I thought I would suffocate. But I would have died a happy woman.

Not long after the best moment of my life, everyone gathered their things to call it a night. They all had a long drive back to San Diego, so with one last assembly line of kisses and hugs, I found myself alone. In a new house. With my man.

The wee hours belonged to us.

We chillaxed on the couch, watching ESPN on the 53-inch, all wrapped up in each other. "I had the best time today," I said, tracing my finger around my diamonds. "Then you went and put a big cherry on top. Boy, you are somethin' else."

"I know." That's all he said. Homeboy just knew he was the shiznit. Shoot, I had no doubt, either.

I shifted my head against his chest, cutting my eyelids at him. "Oh, 'you know', huh? You just think you slick."

He rested his head against his armrest of the leather sectional. Those sexy lips curved upward. "Cause I am."

Shoot, I couldn't argue with that. Pretty smooth how he did his thing. I cried a river when he slid the ring on. For real, girl. Elation in my soul made me want to jog around the block, sharing pieces of joy with the world.

I stared at my ring for the umpteenth time. "So, how long have you been planning this?"

He hit the Mute button on the big screen's remote. "For a few weeks. Didn't want to get everybody together until Baby Boy got off deployment. Damn, now you got me calling him that!"

I chuckled. Snuggling my back against his chest, I wrapped his arm under my two babies. "And you mean to tell me everyone knew but me?"

"Yup."

"Can't believe nobody slipped up, especially Charlotte. Looks like keeping secrets is your specialty, huh?"

He chuckled. "Well, you know," he said, stroking his chin, "I had to do my thang."

"You definitely did that."

He traced a finger around my chin. I peeled my stare away from my diamonds and turned to my husband-to-be. He said, "Are you sure you're okay with driving to and from San Diego? That's an hour commute each way just to get to work. I know you've been doing it a few months already, but you think you can do it everyday?"

"Of course, Boo. Why?"

He shrugged. "I don't know. Kinda worried me that the distance would wear you down."

Damn, I love this man! I thought. *Always makes me number one!*

"Baby," I said, caressing his cheek, "I think I've already proven that I'm willing to do it." We kissed.

"Good. You know I wasn't going to stay in this new two-thousand square-foot house by myself every night, so take a good look. This is our home now. Once your apartment lease ends, you belong here."

I threw up a fake salute. "Yes, sir!"

Our home. I repeated those words in my head. *Our home.* Until he said that, I guess my new reality hadn't dawned on me. I glanced at my ring. This was our home! Home of a future husband and wife. Nothing sounds sweeter.

My King raised himself up. I slid my butt against the cushions so he could stand.

He said, "I think I'm ready to break in that hot tub. You with me?"

"Shoot, you don't have to ask me twice. I'll be there in a bit."

"All right." He leaned down and massaged his mouth and tongue against mine. Gave me a wet, slobbery lip-lock to make damn sure my butt wouldn't take too long.

While I got my bearings straight, he grabbed the ends of his tank top and eased it over his head. My eyes dropped. Damn, those ripples. Aw, those pecs.

Oh, it's on tonight, I thought. He turned and I watched him walk toward the gazebo outside.

Lawd. Ain't that a trip? There I was, slumped against the couch, staring at the ceiling fan, a smile stapled so hard to my face I couldn't erase it even if I tried.

I turned my head to a corner table and gazed at a picture of me in Palm Springs between Baby Boy's diploma and my degree. Damn, seemed like yesterday, but a lot has changed in a year. Charlotte and Greg are parents now, with Greg about to publish a book. Baby Boy's sister Shanda is an A and B business student in college with a fine-as-hell pre-med boyfriend named Craig. Tammy and Terrell are our two new couple friends, now. And Baby Boy—my nickname for Daryl's little brother Donald, with that cutie-booty baby face and all—is in the Navy, home after a six-month deployment with a girlfriend named Lorraine.

Shoot, even me! No way in the world did I envision myself engaged to the man of my dreams. Fate is a wondrous thing, girl.

Oh! Wanna know how I "conquered" the King Dingaling?

Well, I haven't. Shoot, I can't, and I really don't want to, either. That thing is not to be dominated. Obviously, I haven't pounced on it and ruptured my insides since Palm Springs; I know to approach the King with extreme caution. And Daryl makes sure to love me down with slow, smooth strokes.

And that's quite all right with me. Of course, he positions himself with a large gap between us to avoid rammin' that thing through my shoulder blades and shit. Gotta take necessary precautions, ya know.

"Chelle!" Daryl yelled from the gazebo, "Where you at, babe?"

I pressed the power button on the TV remote and jumped up from the couch. "I'm comin'!"

As I skipped my happy butt outside, the sight of Daryl's rock hard physique bathed in moonlight slowed my pace.

"Damn, damn, damn," I said.

I stood in the doorway and folded my arms. Didn't want to move for a moment. Just wanted to view natural beauty at its best. I could've been standing in front of Niagara Falls, the Grand Canyon, blue oceans of the Caribbean—whatever. None of them compared to the awe of my tall, cut-up, dark-skinned lover man flaunting a twelve-in-a-half inch weapon guaranteed to wallop my brain cells.

He wore that familiar naughty grin.

I swiped my tongue across my lips.

"So," he said, placing his hands on his hips, "you ready to christen this hot tub?"

My eyes dropped to King Dingaling, then went back up to meet his gaze. "Oh yeah. Most definitely."

"Well, Mrs. Jackson-to-be. I have one question."

"And what's that?

"Do you think you can handle this?"

Can I handle that? Shoot, he ain't said nothin' but a word. Time to get dir-tay up in here.

So, there it is, girl. That's my story.

What?

C'mon, now. You know I was joking about kicking Daryl to the curb, right? No way in the world I'd be dumb enough to let that man go. I hit the "blackpot." Dump that?

Hell no!

A foot-long penis attached to a beautiful employed man who owns a house! Hel-lo? You do the math.

That's like giving away the winning lottery ticket! And you know black folks don't hit the lottery that often!

C'mon, a sista ain't stupid. Daryl and I will start a whole new chapter and, best believe, I plan to make what we have a bestseller!

Now, if you'll excuse me, "booty" calls. ;)

The End

Book Club Questions

1. Reject #1 Gerald tried to "stick things in spots that didn't belong." Would you say it's common for some men to try and make a woman explore sexuality in ways that may be uncomfortable for her (for example, strange sexual positions, public sex, sex on camera, etc)?

2. Reject #2 Lawrence was packing an extra belly button at best. Is it true when someone says "it's not the size of the bat; it's how you swing it?" Is it possible to be happy with a short-short man, even if he has all the necessary qualities you want in a partner?

3. Reject #3 Gene took being natural to asteroid levels, sometimes showering only a few days a week and not brushing his teeth every day. Have you ever encountered a man like him? Could you be open-minded and date a man like Gene?

4. Michelle meets Daryl and was so attracted to him she almost gave it up on the first "date" in Daryl's apartment. If Daryl hadn't stopped her, she would have. Could an attraction be so strong that it's okay to sleep with someone on the first date?

5. Is it unrealistic to believe a hot-blooded man would deny himself a chance at a one-night stand? Would a man typically deny sex under any circumstance?

6. After her phone call with Charlotte, Michelle grew suspicious of Daryl. Is it common for women to try and dig up dirt on a man who seems too good to be true (Google searches, stalking him at his job, etc)? Are women constantly looking for the other shoe to drop if things are going well in a relationship?

7. Daryl revealed his secret weapon to Michelle in their Palm Springs resort hotel room. On the flipside: Is it possible to stay committed to a man who is too large and can literally split a woman when intimate every time—especially during wild, "jungle" sex?

8. Do you think there are handsome men who are tired of the club scene and want to settle down—but are packing a third leg? Is it possible for a well-hung man to even want to settle down?

9. We often read about men who proudly reveal their "tree trunks" like a superhero in a costume and can do it from sun up until sun down. Yet, Daryl was self conscious and didn't want to reveal his "gift" to Michelle until he was absolutely ready, which is why it took him weeks. Did his awkward nature spin a unique perspective on men who are hung?

10. Did you like/dislike the conversational tone of the story?

11. What were the most memorable scenes?

12. Overall, did you enjoy the book? Would you recommend it?

The Two Minute Drill:

A Lesson for the Guys, A Little Insight for the Gals ☺

"I hit it from breakfast, through lunch up until dinner, man! Beat it up all night long!"

Oh, boy. You've heard something like this before, right? Someone of the male persuasion (a friend, maybe even yourself?) talking about how he had some girl crawling up the walls from super human hump action. Yeah, right. I'm a hot-blooded man, too. And I know that during most rump sessions we men tend to have two-minute alarm clocks.

Now, before the PC police come after me, I understand some men have genuine physical problems. "Misfires," if you will, a real need for the blue pill. I'm not talking about them, though. I'm referring to the Super Freaks, always bragging about lasting longer than back-to-back showings of the movie Titanic. Got the "sword" skills of a Samurai.

And speaking of "sword," I'd bet these fools have a nickname for their buddy down south, right? Probably something like "Herminator" or "Big Willie." Sounds about right? I got one, too ... but I'll, uh, keep it to myself.

Despite Big Willie's talent, though, you sing a different tune once you sample the goodies because that private sector between a woman's thighs is mmm-mmm good. Delicioso. Literally turns a man's brain to mush. What's that saying? You spend nine months trying to get out of it, but the rest of your life trying to get back in? So true.

Meanwhile, we men know three things: Lock, load, fire! All in about the time it takes a microwave to heat popcorn. And you know I speak the truth. Hell, the two-minute alarm clock probably sounded off on you last night, huh? C'mon, don't lie. I know the scenario by heart through sorry experience. It goes something like this:

You're in front of her, inches from the pearly gates that lead to paradise. She lies spread-eagle. That's unrestricted access to do whatever you want. She pushes the remote control away to focus on you, but the TV stays on. Don't matter. Can't hear it anyway because TV light glows off your lady's naked skin, clouding your senses. Your gaze seizes on the cocoa/caramel/butterscotch/vanilla—-whichever applies—flavored figure lying on her back. She adjusts her head against the pillow, swipes hair away from her dark eyes. So damn sexy, her feline grace. Nothing compares to a beautiful woman's birthday suit. Like chicken soup for the "pole."

Buttermilk smooth legs are bent up, wide open at the ready, field goal style. And you're in the red zone. Time to give your girl a piece of the rock.

Time: zero seconds.

And so you slither inside ... slow ... digging into your personal crawl space. Her sweet lips kiss, suck, then swallow Big Willie, deep-throat style. Half-way in, you gasp. She gasps. Or curses. Don't matter. You drop your eyelids, allow your mind to plug into the Matrix-like sensation of your woman's channel. Her back arches until her spine loops, legs become wings, two become one, until...

Uh-oh. It's a different ball game now. Of course, if you claim to be a Daddy Whip King it won't take Herculean strength to keep from popping the cork off your "bottle" within two minutes. But nine times out of ten, you'll deflate faster than a tire with a 10-inch puncture. And you're on the clock.

The dance begins. In the driver's seat, you ride first gear. I think you know what I'm talking about. Slow, deep dips and circles inside your lady's ocean. That's right. Why rush? She rocks with you, same rhythm, same speed.

Time: Forty seconds.

With each stroke, you witness her steady transformation from civilized to barbaric. Manicured nails jab your lower back. Her erratic moans mix with curse words. Such a nice tune. Your favorite song.

Your lady's vocal chords become a siren, howling like a fire truck speeding toward a 2am fire. Dribble smacks your forehead. Deeper. *Deeper!* And that's what you do ... then ...

Thump! What was that? Oh, nothing big. Just you knocking the remote control onto the hardwood floor. Takes more than a broken remote to cease-fire, though. Nothing can disturb this groove.

Instead, you open your eyes; a sly grin creeps across your cheeks. Parting her mouth, your lady swipes her tongue along a pair of lips riper than strawberries.

Man ... that blissful look she has—a glow. That's all you, playa. Natural beauty manipulated by "penile" power, twisting her face like rubber. Damn, got her looking like plastic surgery gone wrong. But slow down. Pay attention to those tiny tingles in your gut. *I can hold it,* you say in your head. Yeah, right. 2nd gear.

No, no. 4th gear.

Time: One minute.

Bedsprings squeak. The headboard beats the wall. With her legs wrapped around you, her ankles handcuff just above your butt bone. Oh, boy—she got you on lockdown, now. Under her vice-grips, Big Willie nearly drowns in her parted seas.

Time: One minute, fourteen seconds.

She slaps her hands against your butt. No longer a lady, your woman becomes "animal" now. Forget the Barry Manilow soft stuff— it's time to get Billy Idol on that ass until her whole body rebel yells. Or so you think.

Time: One minute, thirty seconds. 5th gear.

She latches onto the back of your head, stabs her tongue in your mouth. Your faces become a smeared glob of saliva and sweat, but between deep moans, muffled curse words and tongue-fu, your woman cries your name and screams, "give it to me!" And you oblige.

Actually, you try.

As your woman gnaws a path toward spasmodic oblivion, tingles within your scrotum have become a beehive, mushrooming into an explosion bound to exorcise your stamina.

"Oh, damn," you whisper. *"Not now!"*

Oblivious to your turmoil, your lady yells, "Yes! *Yes!*" Her legs have clamped tighter; you're a nut, she's a nutcracker. The siren cries drown the voices in your head, begging you to hold strong. You put up a good fight ... somewhat. Easing Big Willie back to stifle eruption, you then attempt mind-over-matter tricks:

Mr. Van Johnson, your fourth-grade teacher, digging up his nose. Nasty. Then the nursery rhymes begin, like the little old lady that lived in a shoe. Humpty-dumpty sitting on the wall. Little Miss Muffet sitting on a tuffet, eating her curds and whey. Dumb strategy, I know. You learned these diversion tactics from your sexpert buddies. Doesn't work, though. You're too busy grunting like a pig with grass stuck in its throat.

Then the "lid" pops open. Uh-oh.

With a deep, hard thrust, little soldiers bumrush toward freedom. One squirt ... then two. A cuss word later, you gasp, skin stretches around your neck and then...

Splash. Friction has milked the cow.

Houston, we have a problem.

Now if married, your mini warriors scatter like roaches with the lights turned on. If playing the field, I hope they slam headfirst into a rubber hat.

Okay, so now what? All stop. As you pancake your girl, heaving in loads of air while smothering her, a five-second pause sets in. Then your woman says three words no man wants to hear: "No. You. Didn't!"

Yes, I did, you say in your head.

What happened? Twenty-four seconds into last gear and your gasket sprung a huge leak.

I know what happened: Did you really want to evacuate the premises? Especially while riding a euphoric rush? I didn't think so.

And your time? One minute, fifty-four seconds. Beat your record from the night before. But don't feel so bad. You can get around this! Did you know 88% of men have run the same two-minute sprint at least once? You're in good company. Happens to the best of 'em.

At this point, however, I suggest you blow Big Willie back up or go "tongue-surfing." Don't leave your woman hanging like that! Keep her fire burning until she reaches the apex like you did so damn fast.

You definitely don't want to say something silly like, "damn, baby, that was good," then roll over into unconsciousness wearing a goofy grin.

If you do, a swift kick to the butt will catapult you off the bed face-first onto the floor—right next to that broken remote control.

Then you, Mr. Super Freak, will suffer long and hard—emphasis on "hard"—because your woman will boycott the booty for at least a month. You two-minute tease you.

So you know what to do: If you can't super-size Big Willie fast enough, ya gotta go downtown, so dig in, man! Hope you're hungry!

Also Available from TPC Books

www.ingramcontent.com/pod-product-compliance
Lightning Source LLC
Chambersburg PA
CBHW050323200626
46810CB00022B/1098